Their eyes locked.

It was as simple as that. And as shattering. In that brief moment of contact, Jake's grin faded. The fingers he'd wrapped around her wrist tightened.

Those damned chemical signals coursing through Rachel's system started flashing red alert again. Rising up on tiptoe, she met him halfway.

The kiss was cool at first but heated up fast. Jake fitted his mouth over hers. His hands framed her face. Fingers callused by rope and wire brushed her cheeks.

Everything that was female in Rachel responded to the feel of his corded biceps, his hard mouth, the faint scent of leather and clean, sharp wind that clung to his shirt. And some faint corner of her mind shouted that this was more than just a mindless, hormonal response. That it was Jake who'd found her own trigger.

And only Jake,

Dear Reader,

Once again, we've rounded up six exciting romances to keep you reading all month, starting with the latest installment in Marilyn Pappano's HEARTBREAK CANYON miniseries. *The Sheriff's Surrender* is a reunion romance with lots of suspense, lots of passion—lots of *emotion*—to keep you turning the pages. Don't miss it.

And for all of you who've gotten hooked on A YEAR OF LOVING DANGEROUSLY, we've got *The Way We Wed*. Pat Warren does a great job telling this tale of a secret marriage between two SPEAR agents who couldn't be more different— or more right for each other. Merline Lovelace is back with *Twice in a Lifetime*, the latest saga in MEN OF THE BAR H. How she keeps coming up with such fabulous books, I'll never know—but I *do* know we're all glad she does. Return to the WIDE OPEN SPACES of Alberta, Canada, with Judith Duncan in *If Wishes Were Horses....* This is the kind of book that will have you tied up in emotional knots, so keep the tissues handy. Cheryl Biggs returns with *Hart's Last Stand*, a suspenseful romance that will keep you turning the pages at a furious clip. Finally, don't miss the debut of a fine new voice, Wendy Rosnau. *A Younger Woman* is one of those irresistible stories, and it's bound to establish her as a reader favorite right out of the starting gate.

Enjoy them all, then come back next month for more of the best and most exciting romance reading around—only in Silhouette Intimate Moments.

Yours,

Leslie J. Wainger
Executive Senior Editor

Please address questions and book requests to:
Silhouette Reader Service
U.S.: 3010 Walden Ave., P.O. Box 1325, Buffalo, NY 14269
Canadian: P.O. Box 609, Fort Erie, Ont. L2A 5X3

MERLINE LOVELACE
Twice in a Lifetime

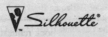

INTIMATE MOMENTS™

Published by Silhouette Books

America's Publisher of Contemporary Romance

 **SILHOUETTE BOOKS**

ISBN 0-373-27141-7

TWICE IN A LIFETIME

MERLINE LOVELACE

spent twenty-three exciting years in uniform as an air force officer, serving tours at the Pentagon and at bases all over the world before she began a new career as an author. When she's not tied to her keyboard, she and her husband enjoy traveling, golf and long, lively dinners with friends and family.

Be sure to look for Merline's novella, "The Major's Wife," part of Harlequin Historical's sizzling anthology THE OFFICER'S BRIDE, on sale next month.

This is for Marie Henderson Lovelace, my friend,
shopping companion and sister-in-law extraordinaire,
who's helped me plot at least a dozen books
during our many travels with our own handsome hunks!

Chapter 1

"Jake?"

Jake Henderson caught his name above the clamor of the Coconino County Fair. Held each Labor Day weekend at the park just outside Flagstaff, Arizona, the fair was in full swing.

The last rays of the September sun slanted down on the crowded midway, exhibition halls and livestock arenas. Shrieks chorused from the Ferris wheel and scrambler, while the loudspeaker boomed the relative merits of Benjamin Miller's entry in the shorthorned bull category. With half an ear tuned to the announcer, Jake glanced over his shoulder.

A pair of lively hazel eyes smiled up at him. More green than brown, they were wide-spaced and intelligent. Hair a deep shade of mink swept back from a slight widow's peak to swing in a silky fall that tipped up at the ends. As Jake stared into a face sculpted by slanting brows, high cheekbones, and a determined chin, the woman's mouth curved.

"You don't recognize me, do you?" Her smile widening, she stuck out her hand. "It's Rachel. Rachel Quinn. Alice Quinn's niece."

"Good Lord!"

Jake took the hand she offered. Her grip was strong. No-nonsense. And warm. A shock of heat traveled up his arm as he wrapped his fingers around hers.

He pitched his voice above the loudspeaker. "The last time I saw you, you were mostly all arms and legs."

She still was, he noted, skimming an eye down a mile-long stretch of tight jeans. The body that went with her killer legs had filled out nicely, though.

Jake hadn't paid any particular notice to a woman's figure in years, but a man would have to be blind or stone-cold dead to miss Rachel Quinn's lush rounded hips and the high breasts that pushed at the front of her cream-colored sweater.

Jake wasn't blind. And only his heart had died.

Releasing her hand, he shoved his straw Resistol hat to the back of his head.

"It must be, what? Eight, nine years since you spent the summer here in Flagstaff with your aunt?"

"Twelve," she corrected. "I had just finished my junior year in high school."

The hazy memory of that long-ago summer surfaced. Jake waited for the round of applause for Benjamin Miller's bull to die before sharing it.

"Best I recall, you left Flagstaff right after you dumped my youngest brother on his butt in a pile of manure and stalked off, swearing you weren't ever going to speak to him again."

"Best *I* recall, Sam deserved dumping on his butt. And I stuck to my guns. I didn't return his phone calls after that particular incident."

A dimple appeared in one of her cheeks.

"Okay, he only contacted me once after he scraped off the horse poop, and the message he left on my aunt's answering machine did *not* invite further conversation."

The lone dimple drew Jake's fascinated gaze. The fleeting thought crossed his mind that Sam might have blown it big time when he let this one get away if a certain package of female dynamite named Molly Duncan hadn't been waiting for him in his future. Molly had shot the youngest of the

five Henderson brothers down in flames during a
fierce battle over an oleander hedge and had kept
him in a permanent state of surrender ever since.

Which is what Jake tried to tell Rachel…in
slightly expurgated terms…when she inquired
about the gangly rancher's son she'd dated that
long-ago summer.

"Sam's married and…."

The loudspeaker boomed again, drowning out his
words.

"What?"

"Sam's married. He and Molly are…."

The announcer waxed poetic about the next entry
in the shorthorned competition. Jake gave up trying
to out-shout him.

"Let's get away from the noise."

With the courtesy Jessie Henderson had alter-
nately preached and pounded into her five sons, he
took Rachel's elbow and steered her toward the
open-air pavilion that formed the heart of the fairgrounds. Strings of colored lights wove an overhead
canopy, winking yellow and red and green in the
coming twilight. Picnic tables ringed the concrete
floor, which had been cleared for the dancing that
would come when the band finished setting up.

Dozens of concession stands surrounded the pavilion and spilled their mouth-watering lures into
the dusk. The aroma of spicy barbecue, sizzling fa-

jitas, buttery popcorn and sugar-sweet cotton candy drew throngs of hungry fair-goers to the various booths.

Claiming an empty table, Jake waited till Rachel had taken a seat on the bench to offer her something to settle the dust of the fairgrounds. "Would you like a beer or a soft drink?"

She eyed the long lines winding around the booths. "I wouldn't mind a beer later, when the lines go down."

Tipping her head back, she caught the red blaze firing the jagged peaks that ringed the city and surrounding countryside. The sun had dropped behind the San Franciscos, setting them aflame.

"Look at that! I'd forgotten how beautiful the sunsets are out here."

Except for a stint in the marines, Jake had spent his entire life in the shadow of the rugged peaks. He didn't spare them a glance. The young woman with her face tilted to the sky provided a more interesting view.

"What brought you back to Flagstaff?"

"Aunt Alice just had a hip replacement. I had piled up some use-or-lose vacation time, so I drove out to stay with her for a month or so while she recuperates."

Although the population of Flagstaff now hovered around forty-five thousand, the northern Ari-

zona city still retained enough of a small-town
atmosphere for Jake to feel a sharp bite of concern.
Alice Quinn had run the café on Aspen Avenue for
three decades and just retired a few years ago. Jake
hadn't heard she'd been hospitalized.

"I didn't know Alice was ailing. I don't get into
town often these days. I'll have to call on her."

"She'd be thrilled. She told me she doesn't see
much of the Henderson boys since they're all
grown up. Or read about them in the local paper,"
Rachel added with mischievous glint in her hazel
eyes.

The laughter that rumbled through Jake's chest
surprised him. He couldn't remember the last time
he'd felt this easy or relaxed around anyone other
than his brothers and their families.

"Well," he drawled, "I admit we managed to
get into our share of brawls and scrapes in our rambunctious youth."

More than their share, according to their long-
suffering mother, their often exasperated father and
the county sheriff who'd hauled each of the Henderson boys home in his squad car at various times
in their exuberant youth.

Big John Henderson was dead now and Jessie
Henderson had moved off the Bar-H into a condo
in Sedona, some fifty miles south, but Jake still
maintained an active relationship with Buck Silver-

thorne, Coconino County's deputy sheriff. You couldn't run a twenty-thousand-acre spread and lease another thirty thousand from the government without regular contact with the law. Drunken hands, missing equipment and the occasional vandalized line shack were all part of the ranching business.

Hooking her elbows back on the table, Rachel tipped her head and studied him through thick, sable lashes. "Do you and your brothers all still live at the Bar-H?"

"No, just me. Evan—he's nearest to me in age— is an assistant U.S. district attorney. He and his wife, Lissa, live in San Diego."

"I remember him. Vaguely." Her forehead crinkled. "Wasn't he a motorcycle nut?"

"He still is, although his career and Lissa's keep them off the roads more than either one of them likes. She's a recording artist," Jake explained. "Gospel songs, primarily."

He tossed off a few of his sister-in-law's latest hits, but Rachel confessed she wasn't familiar with gospel music. Jake hadn't listened to it much, either, before Evan brought Melissa Marie James back to the Bar-H to face the hordes of reporters waiting to devour her. Now...

Now, he filled some of his empty nights with the

soaring hymns his sister-in-law composed and recorded.

"What about your other brothers?" Rachel asked. "Reece, isn't it? And Marsh?"

"Reece is an engineer with the Bureau of Reclamation. He does repair work on dams mostly. His projects take him all over the world. His wife, Sydney, is a documentary filmmaker, so she bundles up their two-year-old son and travels with him. Marsh was a field agent with the DEA until Lauren recently informed him he's going to be a father. He's just traded his gun for a desk."

"And Sam? You said he was married."

Jake paused, not entirely sure how close Rachel Quinn and his brother had gotten that summer. If Sam had followed his usual pattern before Molly cut him off at the knees, he'd probably given Rachel good cause to shove him butt-first into the manure pile. Jake didn't want to stir up old hurts by rubbing Sam's happiness in her face, but a quick glance at her clear, untrammeled eyes convinced him she wasn't nursing a secret longing for his youngest brother.

"Sam's very happily married," Jake confirmed. "He and his wife and daughters live in Albuquerque, where he commands a flight test agency."

"Daughters?" Her winged brows soared. "How many does he have?"

"Three. A four-year-old whirlwind and twins who are just old enough to keep him and Molly hopping."

"No kidding?" She gave a hoot of delight. "Talk about poetic justice! Sam Henderson, the father of three girls. I'd love to see him in harness like that. Or better yet, be a fly on the wall when he tries to advise them on how to handle their dates!"

Still gleeful, she tipped him a smile. "What about you, Jake? How many children do you and…? Sorry, I can't remember your wife's name."

As if a curtain had suddenly dropped, the raucous noise of the crowd faded. Twinkling colored lights dimmed to a blur. The pain Jake had lived with for three endless years lanced straight into his heart.

"Ellen," he murmured, forcing his wife's name.

"That's right. Ellen."

He saw Rachel's lips move. Heard her voice through the ache that reached into his chest, grabbed his heart, and squeezed. Hard.

"How many children do you and Ellen have?"

He could do this. He *had* to do this. He'd drowned his grief in a bottle for too many months. Fought his family's every effort to pull him out of the grave he'd wanted to share with Ellen. Rationally, he knew life had to go on. Intellectually, he recognized the therapeutic value of talking through his loss.

Emotionally...

Emotionally, the memory of the cold, snowy day he'd buried his childhood sweetheart and the wife he'd thought to grow old with still wrapped him in barbed wire.

"We didn't have any children," he answered quietly. "We had hopes we'd be able to start a family when Ellen was killed."

Shock blanked Rachel's features. As if he'd flicked a switch, the liveliness in her face died. Almost as quickly, pity rushed in.

"Oh, no! I didn't know."

Jake felt the walls clanking into place, the door slamming shut. He'd seen that look so often, endured the embarrassment and stumbling condolences that invariably followed.

Death, he'd learned, wasn't a matter for polite conversation. It made most folks uncomfortable. Even worse was the quick change of subject that invariably followed. It was as if Ellen had never existed. As if the fact that she'd died had somehow made even her name anathema among the living. That hurt almost as much as the aching sense of loss that stayed just under his ribs.

To his surprise, Rachel didn't fumble for words

or turn the subject. Her eyes filling with compassion, she reached for his hand.

"I'm so sorry, Jake."

The soft murmur reached him on the first strains of a two-step. The band had finished setting up and tuning their instruments. A bass guitar strummed a lead. Moments later, a smoky-voiced vocalist crooned into the mike. With the weepy country ballad providing a counterpoint to the music that pumped from the midway, Rachel searched his eyes.

"Can you tell me what happened, or does it hurt too much to talk about it?"

He hesitated, measuring how much of the brutal truth she could take. All of it, he decided. His impression of the grown-up Rachel Quinn more than matched that of the skinny, scrappy teenager who'd tangled with Sam.

"Ellen was killed in a drive-by shooting down in Phoenix three years ago. The intended victim passed through the intersection a half second before she did. He survived the murderous crossfire. She didn't."

"I'm so sorry," Rachel said again. "I don't remember her very well, but I do recall how happy you two seemed. You... You must miss her terribly."

As much as a man would miss breathing.

"Yeah," he said evenly, "I do."

She gave a small nod, and Jake tucked away his memories. He'd pull them out later...or they'd pull him.

"What about you? Have you shoved any more men into manure piles since Sam?"

The smile crept back into her eyes. "A few. You don't find a whole lot of keepers in my line of work."

"What do you do?"

"I'm a safety analyst with the National Transportation and Safety Board."

An analyst with the NTSB. That was probably the last profession Jake would have guessed. With her tall, trim build and healthy tan, Rachel looked like she spent considerably more time outdoors than inside an office, hunched over a computer keyboard or stacks of reports.

"How did you get into that line of work?" he asked, intrigued.

"My undergraduate degree's in materials science."

Jake hadn't grown to manhood in a state that still derived a large percentage of its income from mining without knowing that materials science included everything from metallurgy to manufacturing. When he said as much, Rachel nodded.

"I did a lot of work with metal fatigue and

X-ray diffraction before I specialized in composites. Since they're used so much today to manufacture automobiles and aircraft, it tied right in with my job. I do lab work mostly, at the NTSB lab in Washington, D.C.''

"D.C.'s a big city," Jake commented, going back to their earlier discussion. "I would have thought you'd find a bucketful of keepers in pin-striped suits and power ties."

"Well, there's one with definite potential."

"I don't imagine he liked the idea of you taking off for Arizona for a month."

Jake had thrown out the comment more to make conversation than anything else, but Rachel's glance strayed once more to the slowly darkening peaks.

"He's not real happy about it," she admitted, "but Aunt Alice needed me and I needed some time to think things through."

Uh-oh. Trouble in paradise. He recognized the signs even as she swung her gaze back and gave him a rueful smile.

"Strike that last comment, will you? I wouldn't want it to get back to my aunt. She has enough on her plate right now without worrying about my love life…such as it is."

"Consider it struck."

A companionable silence drifted down between

them. Once again, Jake was surprised at how easy
it was to talk…and not talk…to Rachel Quinn. He
sprawled with elbows planted on the table behind
him, boots crossed at the ankle. Lazily, he watched
the couples circling under the colored lights. Most
of them danced western style, with the men's arms
either draped over their partners' shoulders or
clasped loosely around their waists.

"That looks so uncomfortable," Rachel commented idly. "All that weight on the woman's
shoulders."

"You've never tried it?"

Her eyes twinkled. "Sam didn't take me dancing
on either of our two dates and we don't have a lot
of country-western bars in D.C."

"Well, you can't go back East again without
learning the two-step. Come on, I'll show you."

Jake realized his mistake the moment he guided
Rachel into the crowd of dancers. Sitting beside her
on a picnic bench and talking was one thing. Sliding her hands up to lock around his neck while he
looped his around her trim waist was something
else again.

She fit him as if they'd been measured and cut
from the same cloth. With his six-feet-plus of lean
muscle, he'd always towered over his elfin wife.
Dancing with Ellen had required minor acts of con-
tortion on his part and careful concentration so he

didn't run her legs off. Not that Jake had minded. He'd always believed that shielding and protecting Ellen was the primary reason the Good Lord had put him on this earth. Still, he had to admit it felt good to hold a woman who could lift her eyes to meet his without craning her neck and whose mouth was within easy kissing distance.

And Rachel Quinn's mouth was eminently kissable.

Guilt slashed into Jake, lightning fast and razor sharp. What the hell was he doing, comparing Rachel to Ellen? Why was he staring down at the woman's soft, ripe mouth? He had no business registering the swell of her hips beneath his palms. No business breathing in the soft, cottony scent of her cream-colored sweater. He would have grunted an apology and walked off the floor right then if she hadn't looked up at him with a laughing challenge in her brown-flecked green eyes.

"Okay, I'm ready as I'll ever be. Just go easy on me. Washington-based safety analysts aren't particularly noted for their two-stepping skills."

It was only a dance, Jake told himself savagely as he moved her into the music. A few turns around the open-air pavilion. Rachel was an old friend. Not even a friend, just an acquaintance. Teaching her a rudimentary two-step didn't constitute an act of disloyalty to Ellen.

None of which explained the shock that jolted through him when another couple bumped into his partner and threw her against him. He felt the impact at every point her body indented his. Despite his rigid determination not to react to the breasts pressed into his ribs or the hips canted against his, his muscles tightened. Locking his jaw, Jake dropped his arms and stepped back.

"This was a mistake."

"I'm sorry?"

She glanced up, obviously startled by his precipitate withdrawal. His shrug was intended to defuse the awkward situation.

"The floor's too crowded to show you the proper moves. Why don't we get that beer I promised you?"

Rachel said nothing as her partner led her off the floor. She had a good idea why he'd pulled back so unexpectedly. She'd felt it, too. The sudden sizzle. The burst of heat that snapped along her nerves.

Her reaction to Jake Henderson took her by complete surprise. She hardly knew him. Until this moment she'd thought of him only as Sam's brother. He was older than her, probably thirty-six or -seven. Not a vast difference when compared to her twenty-nine, but the age gap had seemed huge years ago when she'd first met him.

He carried his maturity with a rugged attractiveness, she had to admit. She slanted him a glance, admiring the silvery glints in the black hair showing beneath his straw hat. She admired, too, the character lines carved into his tanned skin by sun and wind and years of hard-learned experience. Or maybe those lines had sprung from grief. He'd taken the loss of his wife hard. Rachel hadn't missed the stark emptiness in Jake Henderson's face before he closed it down.

The man intrigued her...and stirred her intensely, both of which surprised the heck out of Rachel. She'd intended to use these weeks in Arizona to sort through her feelings for the smart, ambitious congressional staffer she'd dated on and off for almost a year now. The realization that Dale had never struck sparks in her blood so fast or so furiously didn't exactly settle her nerves.

They jumped even more at her first glimpse of the fifty-dollar bill Jake dug out of his wallet and tossed down on the counter of the refreshment booth to pay for her beer and his soft drink. When the concessionaire held the crisp new note up to the light to check it, her heart almost careened out of her chest.

"Just can't get used to these new bills," he grumbled. "The durned pictures are off center. Drives me crazy, the way they printed these things."

Rachel couldn't breathe, didn't dare move. Her eyes locked on the serial number, clearly visible in the light spilling from the booth. She identified the first few digits in the sequence instantly.

They were from a run of newly printed banknotes that were lost when a DC-10 went down in a blinding snowstorm almost a year ago. The cargo plane had been ferrying, among other things, a shipment of newly printed bills from the Bureau of Engraving plant in Fort Worth to the Federal Reserve Bank in Denver.

Rachel had been one of the NTSB representatives on the task force the government and various private concerns convened to determine the cause of the accident. Her analyses of the damage to the composite materials comprising the underbelly of the DC-10 had helped corroborate the fact that a cargo hatch had blown and created unexpected drag. Moments later, the pilots had lost control of their aircraft and flown it into a mountain.

None of the forty million dollars in new bills aboard the plane when it took off from Fort Worth had ever been found or put into circulation...until sixty seconds ago, when Jake Henderson plunked down that fifty.

Chapter 2

Rachel's first instinct was to snatch the banknote away from the concessionaire and wave it under Jake's nose with a fierce demand to know where in blue blazes he'd gotten hold of it.

Her second was to clamp her mouth shut.

She'd spent months on the task force investigating last year's crash. A whole vegetable soup of government organizations had contributed both personnel and expertise to the effort. The NTSB, the FAA, the Departments of Treasury and Transportation, the FBI, the Secret Service and dozens of other agencies had participated in the exhaustive investigation. If Rachel hadn't learned anything else

from the short, stocky FBI agent who'd assumed
control of the investigation when they began to suspect foul play, it was to report any and all leads
and keep *everything* absolutely confidential.

Even the press hadn't been alerted to the fact the
commercial cargo plane was carrying a shipment of
newly printed bills, or that the sealed Bureau of
Engraving container had been dropped from the
plane some time before it crashed. After exhaustive
on-site investigations and reconstruction, the evidence indicated one of the four crew members
killed in the crash had deliberately blown the cargo
hatch and ejected the container. The assumption
was that he'd intended to follow the container
through the hatch and parachute to safety.

If so, he hadn't made it. All four crew members
were still aboard when the DC-10 plowed into that
snow-shrouded mountain. To this day, the investigators hadn't been able to determine whether the
dead crew member had worked alone or had ac-
complices positioned in the vicinity of the drop.
Rachel and Russ Taggart, the lead FBI agent on the
task force, had argued over that one, as they'd argued over several of the initial findings. Russ had
finally conceded that her analyses had thoroughly
substantiated the theory of an accomplice. The idea
that Jake Henderson's fifty-dollar bill might finally

lead the authorities to that accomplice sent Rachel's blood racing through her veins.

With a last glance at the bank note the concessionaire tucked into his cash drawer, she accepted a plastic cup filled to the brim with foaming beer. Her thoughts tumbled fast and furious as she and Jake wove their way back through the crowd. Others had claimed their table, so they stood at the edge of the pavilion. Jake nursed his soft drink and watched the dancers. Rachel barely noticed the cold brew sliding down her throat or the couples whirling around the floor.

"Sam and the rest of the gang are coming home to help with the fall roundup."

Lost in her thoughts, she only half heard Jake's comment. "Excuse me?"

"Sam's coming back to the Bar-H next week to help bring the spring calf crop down from the high pastures. If you want to see him in action, you should drive out for a visit."

"I've seen him in action, remember?"

He smothered a grin at the tart response. "I meant with his girls. You said you couldn't picture him in harness. It's a sight worth seeing."

"Oh. Right. I'll, uh, have to make it out to the Bar-H."

Sam Henderson didn't hold an iota of interest for Rachel right now. Her one thought was to get to a phone. Russ Taggart worked out of the FBI's Denver office. He'd probably jump the first plane to Flagstaff in the morning.

Tipping back her head, she downed the rest of her drink in a few healthy swallows, then tossed the cup in a trash container. "It was good seeing you again, Jake. Thanks for the beer. Maybe we can finish the dancing lesson some other time."

"Maybe."

"I've got to go," she said with a breezy smile. "See you around."

Jake tipped two fingers to his hat brim and said nothing as she walked away. He didn't blame her for tossing down her beer and lighting out like a mare who'd just smelled snake. He'd all but shoved her out of his arms a while ago, and had barely pushed two words through his mouth since. No doubt she was as anxious to get shed of him as he was to see her gone. He didn't like the prickly heat she'd raised on his skin…or the way his eyes followed her as she cut a path through the crowd.

She moved with the easy, long-legged grace of a woman content with herself and her lot in life. Her pulled-back hair swayed with each step. The seductive movement drew more than one admiring male glance, as did her curvy, jean-covered rear. She looked as good from the back as she did from the front.

Too damned good.

Cursing under his breath, Jake wrenched his gaze away. He wasn't a fool. Nor was he dead from the waist down. The fact that he'd buried his heart with Ellen didn't necessarily keep his testosterone from spiking occasionally. It was a normal reaction, a healthy male's response to an attractive female. Nothing he couldn't shrug off.

To his annoyance, the shrugging took more effort than he anticipated. Rachel Quinn lingered in his mind long after he took a last stroll through the livestock barn, quit the fair, and climbed into his pickup for the ride out to the Bar-H. The more he thought about the way she'd fit into his arms, the more guilt pricked at him, needling his skin like the hairy spikes of the cholla cactus that grew in the canyons to the south. Locking his jaw, he turned Rachel out of his head and filled the empty void with the woman he'd loved all his life.

He'd probably fallen for Ellen the same day he'd given six-year-old Danny Westerhaze a bloody nose for picking on the tiny, shy blonde who sat in the third row of their second-grade class. From that time on, Ellen Newhope had always considered Jake Henderson her protector. They'd started dating in junior high, got serious in high school, tried to

put things on hold while Jake finished college and
pulled a stint in the marines.

His father had wanted him to see something of
the world, his mother to gain a little sophistication
and hone off a few of his rough edges, but Jake
couldn't wait to shed his uniform and return home
to Ellen. They'd married a week after his discharge
and moved into the ranch house with Big John and
Jessie and those of his brothers who were still at
home.

Big John had signed over five thousand acres and
a hundred head of cattle to give them their start,
which Jake had managed while working with his
father and younger brothers on the family spread.
He'd taken on more and more responsibility as his
brothers left to pursue various careers, then became
majority stockholder and general manager of the
Bar-H after his father's death.

Two years later his mother moved to Sedona.
Jake hadn't understood her abrupt decision at the
time. The Bar-H was Jesse Henderson's home.
She'd lived there all her married life, raised five
sons in the sprawling adobe ranch house, ridden the
high mountain and deep valley range lands with her
husband and their hands. Jake and Ellen had
pleaded with her to stay, but she'd insisted that
she'd take all her memories with her, and it was
time for her to make new ones.

With his arm wrapped around Ellen's shoulders, Jake had watched his mother drive off. For the first time, he and Ellen had the house all to themselves. Jake had marked the occasion by spreading a Navajo blanket on the floor in front of the living room fireplace, peeling off his wife's clothes, and making slow, delicious love to her in the middle of the sunny afternoon.

The years that followed had been good, Jake recalled, his hands gripping the steering wheel. Even the hard times, when drought dried up the grazing lands and late summer hailstorms had destroyed the hay crop. With his other brothers returning home as often as they could to help, Jake and Ellen had ridden out the lows and coasted through the highs.

Then she'd driven down to Phoenix to visit her old college roommate and come home in a coffin.

Jake's knuckles went white. The empty stretch of asphalt ahead disappeared into darkness. After three long years, the memory of his wife's funeral still ripped him apart. And the thought of the ranch house she'd filled with her presence, now waiting dark and quiet, started a tremor snaking its way down his back. With everything in him, Jake ached to slam on the brakes, turn the pickup around, head back into town, and hit the nearest bar.

He'd gone down that road once, though. Came close to never finding his way back. He wouldn't do that to himself...or to Ellen's memory...again. Gritting his teeth, Jake hit the window button and let the night air slap at his face and chest.

The September chill had raised goose bumps on his skin by the time the pickup's headlights found the gravel track leading to the Bar-H. A tin sign with cutouts of rambling cattle surrounding an oversized "H" hung from the wooden crossbar over the road.

After rattling over the cattle guard, the truck wove through the scruffy live oak and piñon to the cluster of buildings nestled in the swell of the foothills. The Bar-H had started small and grown considerably over the years. Stables, tractor barns, tool sheds, two bunkhouses and a guest casita all framed the two-story main house.

The house was constructed in the tiered pueblo style of the Anasazi who'd settled in the region, then disappeared without a trace some five hundred years ago. Massive lodgepole pine beams supported the upper floors. A low-walled adobe fence curved around to a tiled patio that caught the sun in the morning and cool shadows in the afternoon. The sight of a dusty Jeep Cherokee SUV parked in the front drive considerably loosened the knot in Jake's gut. He was grinning as he walked through the front door into the red-tiled hall.

"Unkl Jake!"

His two-year-old nephew barreled out of the great room and raced down the hall as fast as his chubby legs would propel him. Growling like a hungry bear, Jake swung the boy up and tossed him high into the air. The child's shrieks brought his parents ambling out to observe the ritual uncle and nephew had firmly established when Matt was just a few months old.

"Better watch out," Reece drawled. "The little devil stuffed down the better part of the chocolate cake Martina left on the kitchen counter. A few more tosses like that and he's liable to puke all over you."

"Wouldn't be the first time I've been puked on," Jake tossed back. "By him or his father."

"Oh, really?" Sydney Scott Henderson dodged her airborne son to plant a kiss on Jake's cheek. "Is this one of the family stories, or something best left between brothers?"

Tucking the giggling Matthew under his arm like a sack of potatoes, Jake hooked his hat on the ant-lered rack above the hall console and filled his sis-ter-in-law in on the details.

"Reece was about eight, Sam only five when they discovered a box of Cuban cigars Big John had hoarded for years. Of course the idiots decided to help themselves. I found them that night in the toolshed, green as new grass. I managed to get them outside just in time, but it took me an hour to clean my boots the next morning."

"Oh, Lord," Sydney groaned, eyeing her squealing offspring. "Is that the kind of thing I have to look forward to when this one grows up?"

"If you're lucky," Jake replied, tossing Matt ceiling-ward once more. "I could tell you a dozen other stories about his father that would curl your hair."

"I like her hair just the way it is, thanks," his brother drawled.

When the small troop made their way back to the living room, Reece tugged his wife down beside him on the sorrel leather sofa that wore a patchwork of spur scars and heel marks. Stretching out his size twelves on the scarred oak-plank coffee table, he curled Sydney into his curve of his shoulder.

Satisfaction hummed through Reece as the familiar sights and scents embraced him. The huge square table had squatted right where it was for as long as he could remember, a handy platform for boots, books, cattlemen's magazines, half-whittled tree roots, unfinished science projects and whatever else the family happened to drop there. The crossed branding irons had hung over the fireplace since the day the then ten-year-old Evan had mounted them.

Ellen hadn't changed a picture or moved a chair when her mother-in-law left, wanting Jake to feel comfortable in the ranch house he'd always loved. Wanting to keep the place feeling like home, too, to her husband's four younger brothers. Reece's job as a structural engineer for the Bureau of Reclamation had taken him all across the country and to most of the major waterways of the world, yet Ellen had always welcomed him back to the Bar-H with the shy smile that was hers alone.

The memory of her smile brought Reece's gaze back to his oldest brother. They had all taken Ellen's death hard. She had always been there in Jake's shadow, quiet, shy, deferring to him without conscious thought. The Henderson brothers had all grown up thinking of her and Jake as a pair, treating her with the careless affection of a sister. If Reece and the rest of his brothers had wished that she'd take Jake down a peg or two once in a while, maybe shave off a few of those do-it-my-way-or-not-at-all layers, they'd never said so to anyone outside their tight, closed circle.

Only now that he'd found Sydney could Reece even begin to appreciate the devastation Jake must have suffered when Ellen died. The mere thought of drifting off to sleep without his wife's warm body curled up against him put a kink in Reece's gut that wouldn't go away. He couldn't imagine life without her, hoped he'd never see a sunrise or listen to the wind soughing through the pines without hearing her murmur about the incredible sound effect. She'd taught the engineer in him to see the world through her filmmaker's eye. To visualize the poetry in the soaring concrete and earthen dams he worked on and the richness in the often remote civilizations they traveled to. Like Ellen had with Jake, Sydney completed him.

Yet as he observed Jake's rough and tumble antics with Matt, Reece couldn't help wishing his brother would put his grief behind him and find someone else, someone who'd stand up to him occasionally. Rock him back on his heels every so often, the way Sydney did Reece.

That thought was drifting around at the back of his mind when Jake pitched his voice over Matt's giggling screeches to ask if he remembered Rachel Quinn. The question was offhand, but something about the deliberate casualness of it sent Reece's antennas shooting up.

"Rachel Quinn? Is she any relation to Alice Quinn?"

"Her niece. She spent a summer in Flagstaff some years back. Had a thing going with Sam."

"That boy sure does get around," Reece said with an admiring shake of his head. Noting Sydney's sudden frown, he instantly corrected himself. "*Did* get around, before Molly clipped his wings."

With his wife reassured on her sister-in-law's behalf, Reece once again tuned in on his older brother. "So what about this Rachel Quinn?"

"She's back in Flagstaff for a month or so, staying with her aunt while Alice recovers from a hip replacement."

"And?"

Pinning the wildly wiggling Matt to the floor with a big hand, Jake shrugged off the question. "And nothing. I bumped into her earlier tonight at the fairgrounds and just wondered if you remembered her."

"What does she look like?"

"Tall. Dark hair. Nice bu...er, build."

Well, well! As far as Reece knew, this was the first time Jake had noticed a woman's butt since Ellen died. Or admitted noticing it, anyway.

"She couldn't believe Sam's the father of three girls. I invited her out to the Bar-H next week to see the evidence with her own eyes."

"You did, huh?" Reece covered his own sudden spurt of interest in Rachel Quinn with a lift of his broad shoulders. "Hope she comes ready to ride. We can use all the hands we can get. How many extra men does Shad have lined up?"

As it always did when the Henderson brothers got together, the talk turned to the business of the Bar-H. The logistics of searching the high wooded pastures for upwards of six hundred cows, bringing them and their offspring down to the bottom lands, weaning the calves, and loading them on trucks for shipment to feeder operations in Kansas and Oklahoma soon consumed Jake and Reece.

They interrupted their discussion only long enough for Reece to scoop up his son and tote him upstairs to bed. Matt protested volubly every step of the way, of course. It took threats from his father and his uncle's solemn assurance that he'd take him up in the saddle with him tomorrow to get the boy into his Pokémon pj's. By the time the men had accomplished the Herculean task of putting the two-year-old to bed and returned downstairs, Sydney had a pot of coffee brewing and the remains of Martina's chocolate cake served up.

The three of them climbed the stairs again several hours later. As he bid his brother and sister-in-law good-night, Jake experienced the same mix of emotions that always hit him when one of his brothers came home. Genuine enjoyment of their company. Satisfaction in knowing that for a few days the walls would echo with more than just the thud of his own boots and those of the couple who kept the house running. A visceral little pang of envy for their happiness, which he fought like hell but couldn't quite vanquish.

Particularly not with Ellen smiling up at him from the bureau. Jake stood with his shirttails hanging out and half the buttons undone and stared down at the snapshot. It was his favorite, taken a few years after they'd married. She was leaning against a split-rail fence, with a stand of aspen behind her. The leaves were a shiny, liquid gold, almost as bright as her hair. She'd tipped her face to the sun and looked so young. So happy.

Blowing out a ragged breath, Jake turned away. It took only minutes to strip down, minutes more to scrub his face. Then he stretched out in the bed he and Ellen had shared for so many years, crossed his arms behind his head, and watched the shadows dance across the ceiling.

He wasn't even aware that his thoughts had drifted from the slight, dainty blonde he'd married to the tall, confident brunette he'd taken in his arms tonight until he felt himself harden. With a muttered curse, Jake rolled over, punched the pillow, and willed Rachel Quinn out of his head.

Eighteen miles away, a phone shrilled, breaking the silence of the night.

Rachel dived for the instrument on the nightstand in her aunt's tiny guest room. She'd been pacing and prowling for hours, waiting for Russ Taggart to return the call she'd made to the duty officer at the FBI's Denver region headquarters.

"This is Rachel Quinn."

"Taggart here, Rache. It's been a while since I heard from you."

Five months, in fact, since the task force had been formally dissolved and the FBI assumed full responsibility for the still-open investigation.

"The duty officer contacted me and said you wanted to talk. What's up?"

"I spotted one of the bills from Flight 6219."

A stark silence greeted her breathless announcement. Rachel could hear her blood pounding in her ears, sense the sudden tension on the other end of the line.

"When and where?"

"In Flagstaff. Tonight. I'm here visiting my aunt and bumped into an acquaintance at the county fair. He passed a fifty to a concessionaire. I got a glimpse of the serial number, Russ. It's part of the shipment that was aboard the downed DC-10. I'm sure of it."

Taggart's swift reply slashed through her excitement like a saber. "Have you told anyone else about this?"

"No, of course not."

"Don't. Hang on a sec, let me check the airline schedules."

A few clicks of a keyboard later, he came back on the line. "There's a United flight that gets me into Flagstaff at ten-fifteen tomorrow morning."

"I'll meet you at the airport."

"Right. Give me the name of this acquaintance so I can run him through the computers."

"Henderson. Jake Henderson."

"Henderson," Taggart repeated. "Got it. If this character has received so much as a parking ticket in the past five years, I'll soon know about it."

A frown etched between Rachel's brows. In her simmering excitement, she'd formulated a dozen possible scenarios explaining how that bill made its way from the crash site high in the Rockies to Jake's wallet. That he might be anything more than an innocent conduit hadn't figured among the possibilities.

"He's a local, Russ. He's lived in Flagstaff all his life. Someone's obviously passed him the bill."

"There's nothing obvious about it at all," the FBI agent shot back. "I've been working this case for almost a year. At this point, I'm taking nothing for granted, least of all this guy Henderson. I'll run him through the computers."

Chapter 3

"I think you've got it clean enough."

Rachel paused in the act of swiping down the kitchen counter and darted a glance over her shoulder at the woman seated at the knotty pine table. Her aluminum walker was planted close beside her chair.

"I'm sorry. What did you say?"

"You've been scrubbing that countertop for the past five minutes. You're going to take off the Formica finish."

"Oh." Her ready smile popping out, Rachel folded the damp dishrag over the long-necked faucet. "Guess my thoughts were wandering a bit."

"A bit?" Alice Quinn gave a good-natured snort. "They've gone every which way but straight since you got up this morning. Since you got back from the fair last night, now that I think on it."

Cocking a head crowned with an untamable mass of springy, salt-and-pepper curls, she studied her niece's abstracted movements.

"Did you meet up with someone at the fairgrounds?"

Rachel's startled gaze snapped to her aunt. For a moment, she was afraid her thoughts were written all over her face. She'd met up with someone all right, and the results of that meeting had kept her tossing and turning for most of the night.

"Yes," she answered after a moment. "As a matter of fact, I did. Jake Henderson."

"Jake? I haven't seen him in ages. He used to come by the café at least once a week for coffee and a piece of pie when I was still running the place."

"I didn't know Jake's wife was killed a few years ago."

"Didn't I tell you about that?"

"No."

"Terrible tragedy. Just terrible. How did you hear about it?"

"He mentioned it."

"Did he?" Alice's gray brows soared. "Then

you're one of the few people he's talked to about
the shooting. Jake pretty well shut himself up at the
Bar-H after it happened. Don't mix much with his
friends anymore, from what I hear. How's he doing?''

"We only spoke for a little while," Rachel said
slowly, "but my impression is that he's still hurting
for his wife."

"I'm not surprised. Never saw two people more
stuck on each other than Jake and Ellen."

Tucking her hands into the front pockets of her
jeans, Rachel leaned her hips against the counter.
The sunlight slanting through the window above the
sink warmed her shoulders. In the bright glare of
morning, Jake Henderson's image stayed firmly im-
printed in her mind's eye, just as it had for most of
last night.

She hadn't been able to get him out of her head
since her call to Taggart last night. No, that wasn't
quite right. Henderson had chewed up her concentration from the moment he'd taken her in his arms
and ignited small brushfires just under her skin. She
still didn't quite understand how her body could
react so swiftly to the brief contact. Or why she'd
never experienced that smothering rush of heat with
the man she'd been dating off and on for the better
part of a year.

Nor could Rachel figure out why the fact that

she'd sicced the FBI on Jake played so heavily on
her mind. She'd put months of her life into the
crash investigation and subsequent effort to find the
missing forty million dollars. She was as eager as
anyone on the task force to see the case successfully
concluded. Still, she couldn't shake the uneasy feeling that she'd unleashed a pit bull on the unsuspecting Jake.

She'd worked closely enough with Russ Taggart
during those first intense months after the crash.
She knew the agent's short, compact frame housed
a triple A-type personality. He'd driven the entire
task force unmercifully and sent an army of agents
out to track down every lead. In the process, he'd
compiled a huge database that included everyone
from the members of the ground crew who serviced
the downed aircraft to the employees at the manufacturing plant that produced the metal containers
for the ''bricks'' of newly printed bills.

Now Taggart had entered Jake Henderson's
name into his massive database. Once in, Rachel
suspected it would never come out. She knew how
the government bureaucracy worked. She was part
of it herself.

As much as she wanted to solve the mystery associated with the downed aircraft, she couldn't
imagine that Jake constituted anything more than
an innocent and very minor player in the drama. No

doubt someone had passed him the bill. A friend or a business associate. There were probably a dozen or more someones in the string...all of whom Taggart would have to chase down.

Jake was just the first step, Rachel told herself firmly, the jumping off point for the reenergized investigation. An investigation she could contribute to by finding out more about the man, she decided. What better source than Aunt Alice, who'd lived in Flagstaff all her married life and had dished up generous servings of the town's news over the years with every one of her blue-plate specials?

Casually, Rachel refreshed the coffee in the two mugs on the table and reclaimed her chair. Edging aside a pot of cheerful autumn mums, she gently pumped her aunt for information.

"Jake mentioned that Sam and the rest of his brothers are coming home to help with the fall roundup."

"Isn't Sam the one you were so stuck on that summer you stayed with me and your uncle Cal?"

"I wasn't *stuck* on him. He just provided an interesting diversion."

"I seem to recall it the other way 'round," Alice chuckled. "You were the one who diverted him...right into a manure pile."

"He deserved it," Rachel responded lightly, just as she had to Sam's eldest brother last night.

And it was the eldest brother who interested her this morning, not the youngest.

"The Bar-H is a pretty big spread for Jake to run by himself," she continued with studied casualness.

"One of the biggest around," Alice confirmed.

"He must have taken some serious financial hits after the drop in beef prices last year."

"All the ranchers 'round these parts did."

"I've heard that a number of the locals are being forced to sell out to the big conglomerates."

You could hardly spend a week in Flagstaff without hearing dire predictions about the demise of the ranching industry. A bustling university center with a growing high-tech industry, the city still drew twenty-five percent of its tax base from ranching.

Yet so many local cattle operations were being gobbled up by large, multinational conglomerates and wealthy out-of-staters. These distant owners skimmed their profits off the top and put a minimum return back in. It was common knowledge that fewer and fewer Arizona ranchers actually depended on their beef-producing income for their livelihoods. Jake Henderson numbered among that rapidly diminishing minority.

"Any chance Jake might lose the Bar-H?" Rachel asked her aunt.

"There was some speculation about it a while back, but I suspect that boy would chop both hands off at the wrist before he'd sell the Bar-H. His father spent most of his life building the spread up from a scruffy little operation with fewer than fifty cows. Jake's added years of his own blood and sweat to the enterprise, and now runs upwards of six hundred head. The Bar-H is in his blood, in all the boys' blood. They'd do whatever it took to hang on to the place.''

Rachel tapped her finger on the rim of her cup thoughtfully and filed that bit of information away for later reference.

''How did he weather the bad market last year?''

''Word around town is Jake found an infusion of cash to see him through the winter.''

''From where?''

''I don't know. He probably floated some sizeable loans. That's what most of the ranchers who hung on to their spreads had to do.''

She digested that in silence while Alice rambled on about the plight of various friends and neighbors after last year's disastrous market plunge. If Jake had taken out any recent loans, Russ Taggart's computer queries would uncover the exact amounts and due dates. If not...

Her brow furrowing, she traced the rim of her mug with her finger. She had a few hours to kill before she drove out to the airport to meet Russ's plane. Maybe she'd make a few discreet inquiries around town, see what else she could learn.

"I've got to run some errands this morning. Anything you want me to pick up for you?"

"Can't think of a thing, unless you want to swing by the pharmacy and get a prescription refilled for me."

"Sure. Which medication?"

"I'll get the bottle."

"Just tell me," Rachel insisted as Alice reached for her walker.

"Now don't fuss. The doc said I'm supposed to exercise this hip joint as much as possible."

Taking care to keep her right leg outstretched, Alice used the chair arms to lever herself up before transferring her weight to the aluminum walker. One of the physical therapists at the hospital had stenciled her name on the denim pouch snapped to the frame. The convenient little carryall held her aunt's reading glasses, a plastic water bottle, one of the gory thrillers she devoured like candy, and the pills she took to counter her twinges of pain.

Her aunt had bounced back amazingly well from the surgery, Rachel thought as she followed the thumping walker down the hall. The ten days of intensive physical therapy she'd received before being released from the hospital had given her a good start down the path to full mobility. Another week, two at most, and she'd progress from the walker to a cane. At that point, she'd be able to drive again and Rachel could head back to D.C. Assuming, of course, the investigation didn't bust wide open and suck her right in again.

Her…and Jake Henderson.

With that thought buzzing around in her head like a bee with no place to light, she retrieved her purse, cell phone, and car keys from her bedroom.

By the time Rachel wheeled her sporty little convertible into the airport parking lot later that morning, the furrow in her brow had deepened to a distinct crease.

She found an empty spot and sat for a moment, dangling both wrists over the leather-wrapped wheel. The acrid tang of aviation fuel drifted through the air and crowded out the clean, sharp scent of the pines blanketing the mountain slopes around the city. Rachel barely noticed the fumes. Her thoughts were all on Jake.

Damn! She'd had no idea how easy it would be to turn up so many scraps of information about the man. Or what a disturbing picture the bits and pieces would form when quilted together into a whole. All it had taken was a few well-placed questions about the ranching industry, with casual references to Jake sprinkled in here and there.

Hal Tomlinson, her aunt's very friendly and very talkative pharmacist, told Rachel that Jake recently bought his wife's cousin's like-new hay baler. Rather than let it go for pennies at auction when his neighbor was forced to sell out, Henderson paid the top dollar for the baler. Fifteen thousand dollars, Hal recounted. In cash.

When Rachel stopped at the Feed and Grain to pick up more potted mums, Sam Westerby let drop that Jake purchased a champion red Brangus bull a few months back for an undisclosed but reportedly astronomical sum.

The owner of the new and used bookstore who supplied Rachel with a bag of thrillers for Alice mentioned the new truck Henderson had ordered for the Bar-H.

The last piece of information she gathered came from Patty Hall, who trimmed an inch or so off Rachel's shoulder-length, blunt-cut brown mane. The bubbly stylist went into great detail about the annual Fourth of July barbecue Jake and his brothers traditionally threw for their friends and neighbors. This year's feast must have set the Hendersons back a big chunk of bucks, Patty surmised. It was particularly well attended given that it was the first one since Ellen's death…and hosted by the sexiest widower in northern Arizona.

A divorcee of several years standing, the stylist

made no bones about her interest in Jake. She kept close track of his infrequent visits to town and had already heard that he'd danced with Rachel at the fair. Patty interpreted that as a signal that he was finally emerging from his self-imposed isolation and was now fair game.

Jake was fair game, all right. In more ways than one. That fact was confirmed mere moments after Rachel greeted Russ Taggart. Short, athletic and aggressively muscled, the fair-haired FBI agent filed off the plane with the others. His dark eyes took on a glittery sheen when he spotted Rachel.

Shifting his leather carryall to his right hand, he slipped a hand under her elbow and guided her through the milling throng. He waited only until they'd gained the relative privacy of the concourse to share the results of his computer queries.

"On the surface, your boy Henderson looks squeaky clean. Honors graduate of the University of Northern Arizona, promoted to captain during his tour in the marines, past vice president of the Arizona Cattlemens Association. Owns his ranch free and clear. Pays his state and federal taxes on time. No arrests, no outstanding warrants, not even a citation for jaywalking, although he did get hauled before a local judge as a juvie."

"What for?"

"The records were sealed, but I pried the information out of the county clerk. He and his brothers chased down a couple of thugs who'd jumped a friend.''

Rachel had worked with Taggart enough to know he'd never just skim the surface. From the way his eyes gleamed with intensity, he'd found something in Jake's more recent past that had snagged his attention.

"Come on, Russ. Spill it. What other information did you pry loose?''

"Henderson's made some hefty purchases in the past twelve months without dipping into his cash reserves. He's also made two large, unsourced deposits into his operating account.''

"You got into his bank accounts? I thought that took a court order.''

Taggart smiled. "We have our ways, Rache.''

"Right.''

The air around the FBI operative seemed to vibrate. Despite his casual attire of jeans, open-necked white shirt, and a lightweight sports coat, he emanated the same fiercely controlled energy he'd displayed when he'd first taken charge of the task force. He was on the hunt...and this time he'd ID'd a potential quarry.

A queasy sensation swirled in the pit of Rachel's stomach. The idea of Jake Henderson as Taggart's quarry didn't sit well. She couldn't believe he was in any way involved with the lost millions. Okay, she didn't *want* to believe it.

He'd gotten to her last night in a way no other man had. What's more, he was an old friend of her Aunt Alice. Rachel refused to believe her instincts and those of her aunt could have missed the mark so widely.

"No other bills from the missing shipment have popped up," she reminded Taggart. "If Jake deposited a large wad of cash from that run, more serial numbers would have been reported before now."

"Maybe. Maybe not." Weaving through the crowd, Taggart aimed for the rental car desks just beyond the baggage carousels. "The banks in the U.S. Federal Reserve system have been alerted to watch for notes with that particular sequence, but your average clerk handles thousands of bills every day. If Henderson's feeding them in slowly, they could go unnoticed for who knows how long."

Rachel shook her head. "I just don't see it, Russ. He's not the criminal type. Certainly not the kind who'd get involved in a scheme that resulted in the death of four people."

That earned her a hard glance. "Neither was Timothy McVeigh...on the surface."

"I didn't know the Oklahoma City bomber personally," she replied stiffly. "I do know Jake Henderson. One of his brothers is a DEA agent, for Pete's sake. The other is an assistant U.S. district attorney.''

Taggart slowed to a halt, his dark eyes raking over her. ''You said on the phone Henderson was just an acquaintance. Why are you jumping to his defense like this?''

''He's a little more than a mere acquaintance,'' she admitted with a shrug.

''How much more?''

''I dated his brother some years ago.''

''The DEA agent or the attorney?''

''Neither. The youngest one, Sam.''

She had to admit she hadn't reacted to the youngest brother with anywhere near the heat she had to the oldest. Rachel shoved aside the memory of Jake Henderson's lean, muscled frame pressed against her as Taggart reiterated the bottom line.

''The fifty-dollar bill Henderson passed is our only lead to the missing forty million. I'm going to be on him like ticks on a dog.''

''Don't you think you should ask him where he got it before you start painting him as a coconspirator?''

''And alert him to the fact that he's under investigation? Not hardly.''

''Then what's the plan?''

''The computer queries are only the start. I intend

to find out anything and everything there is to know about your boy before I approach him.''

With an exasperated huff, Rachel set the record straight. ''He's not 'my' boy.''

''I stand corrected. Now can we…?''

He broke off as her cell phone pumped out a lively version of ''Ode to Joy.'' Sure that it was Alice wondering what in the world had delayed her, she dragged the instrument out of her purse and flipped up the lid.

''Hello?''

''Hello, Rachel.''

The deep voice certainly didn't belong to her aunt. Talk about timing!

''Hi, Jake.''

Her response lit dark flames in Taggart's eyes. ''Henderson?'' he mouthed.

When she nodded he practically crawled onto her shoulder to listen.

''I got your mobile number from Alice,'' Jake was saying. ''Hope I haven't caught you at an inconvenient time.''

''No. I'm, er, just running some errands.''

''That's what your aunt said.''

A strained silence fell, made even more uncomfortable by the fact that Russ Taggart was listening to every word his unsuspecting quarry uttered.

''Sam called to say he's getting away earlier than

anticipated,'' Jake continued after a moment. "He and Molly are driving in this afternoon with the girls.''

"That's nice,'' she replied inanely.

Honestly, how in the world was she supposed to collect her thoughts with Taggart breathing down her neck and Jake's deep, leather-smooth voice tingling in her ear?

"I thought maybe you and Alice might like to come out to the Bar-H tonight for dinner. You could see Sam in his altered state and I could make amends for not getting into town to visit Alice in the hospital.''

"I, uh…''

"Say yes,'' Taggart hissed.

Shooting him an evil look, Rachel hunched her shoulder. "When you talked to my aunt, did she say whether she felt up to an evening out?''

A smile crept into his voice. "She said she's gone through every mystery novel in the house and has trounced you so many times in gin rummy that you refuse to come back for another beating. She's willing if you are.''

"Well, I…''

"Say yes,'' Taggart ordered again.

"I'd love to see Sam after all these years,'' she finished with another glare at the agent.

"Good. Say around seven?''

"Seven it is."

Rachel had barely flipped the phone shut before the FBI agent rocked back on his heels. A smirk decorated his face.

"Not 'your' boy, huh? From the sound of it, he'd like to be."

"Get real. He invited me *and* my aunt to a family dinner. That doesn't sound like a come-on to me."

Taggart didn't argue the point. "Whatever his reasons for asking you out to his place, it's a great chance for you to nose around."

Once again the ruthless, intent FBI operative, he rapped out a series of terse instructions.

"Keep your eyes and ears open. Get close to the man, draw him out as much as you can. Just don't tip our hand."

Replying tartly that she'd think about it, Rachel left him at the rental car desk.

Taggart watched her stride away, his mind racing. It hadn't stopped churning since her call last night.

Excitement clutched at his insides, rushed through his veins. One of the bills had finally surfaced. At a damned county fair, of all places.

He'd waited months for one to turn up, sweated blood to make it happen. The money didn't matter to him, not anymore, but he knew he wouldn't sleep until he'd tracked that fifty to its source and closed this damned case once and for all. Which is exactly what he intended to do—with or without Rachel Quinn's help.

Chapter 4

Keep your eyes and ears open.

Get close to the man.

Don't tip your hand.

Taggart's instructions sizzled and spit like hot oil in Rachel's mind as she gripped the wheel of her aunt's turquoise and silver '68 Chevy Impala. Like a venerable matron, the chrome-laden sedan rolled majestically along the road that ambled south through silvery scrub and piñon.

Rachel barely noticed high desert landscape or the snow-capped peaks bathed in red-gold glow to her right. Absorbed in her thoughts, she would have missed the turn for the Bar-H completely if her aunt hadn't pointed out the break in the barbed wire. It was marked by a simple arch made of weathered pine poles.

"This is it. My, look at that."

Her niece speared a quick glance at the tin artwork hanging from the wooden crossbar. The metal sculpture depicted a heard of running cattle framed against a backdrop of jagged peaks. Unlike the mass-produced cutouts that had sprung up on farms and ranches throughout the West, this piece had obviously been crafted by an artist. It was probably the work of Jake's sister-in-law. The artsy one. Reece... No, Marsh's wife.

The sedan thumped over the cattle guard. Chewing on the inside of her cheek, Rachel aimed the car down a dirt and gravel road that cut straight west, toward the mountains. With every crunch of the tires, her nerves tightened. She shouldn't have agreed to this dinner. The idea of accepting Jake's hospitality under false pretenses didn't square well with her conscience. The idea of eating his food while she pumped him for information bothered her even more. She was a safety analyst, for heaven's sake. Not a modern-day Mata Hari.

She was also a government employee, she reminded herself sternly, her eyes on the cluster of buildings set almost in the mountains' shadows. She'd performed analysis after analysis on frag-

ments of aircraft components after last year's fatal
crash, probing for clues to what caused it. She had
to get past this guilt for bringing a cloud of suspi-
cion down on Jake. More to the point, she had to
stop obsessing over the jolt of pure, sensual pleasure that had shot through her when he'd taken her
in his arms.

The fair atmosphere had magnified that brief contact all out of proportion, she decided. She was a
sucker for silky cool night air and colored lights,
that's all. Taken in conjunction with toe-tapping
music and the aromas of sizzling fajitas and hot,
buttery corn-on-the-cob, it was no surprise she'd
experienced a sort of sensory spike. With that
thought fixed firmly in her mind, Rachel slowed for
another cattle guard before pulling up at the sprawling, two-story adobe ranch house.

The moment she opened her car door and stepped
into the dusk, her senses spiked again. The evening
air carried the same brisk chill it had last night.
Pinks and reds and golds blazed above the mountain peaks, every bit as colorful as the fair lights.
The honeysuckle that climbed the beamed porch
shading the adobe ranch house put out a scent as
sticky sweet as cotton candy.

There was no way the din that assaulted her ears
could be considered musical, however. Like the
wails of a hundred lost souls, a chorus of mournful

cries rose from portable corrals set up in the open area beyond the barns and sheds. A half-dozen separate pens held calves of white-faced Hereford, black Angus, and a rusty, all-red breed Rachel didn't recognize. The milling calves bawled incessantly, their keening sobs a solid wall of noise.

Wincing at their ear-splitting cries, Rachel slammed her car door and went around to extract her aunt's walker from the back seat. The calves squalled even louder when they spotted the geranium-red shirt she wore with her tan linen slacks. Butting their heads through the corral bars, they added the machine-gun rattle of metal to their pitiful sobs.

"What on earth's the matter with them?" she asked as she helped her aunt out.

"They're missing their mommas," Alice informed her Eastern-bred niece. "They've just been brought in from the pastures and are going through the weaning process before they're shipped off to feeder lots."

"Poor babies!"

"Those 'babies' weigh upwards of four hundred and fifty pounds," was the dry response. "Time for them to be taken off their mama so they can rebuild their strength for the next spring's calf crop."

"A calf a year? Isn't that a little rough on the girls?"

"They wouldn't come into heat if they weren't ready to reproduce. Their hormones tell them when it's time to mate, just as ours do."

Rachel had taken enough biology classes in her science major to appreciate the power of the chemical messengers synthesized and secreted by the endocrine system. She'd never experienced that power with such devastating potency, however, until the front door opened and Jake Henderson stepped out onto the porch.

One glimpse of his tanned, rugged face and Rachel realized she had more in common with a herd of cows than she wanted to admit. Those blasted hormones could really do a number on the female of *any* species. Particularly when a certain male of the same species smiled and came down the front steps with a lean, easy grace to greet his guests.

He must have just taken a shower. His hair was still damp. Rachel had plenty of time to once again admire the dusting of silver in its black sheen while he pitched a friendly greeting over the mewling calves.

"Hello, Alice. Glad to see you're maneuvering so well."

"It takes more than a busted hip to keep me down."

Alice thumped her walker up the flagstone path. Jake's glance swept past her and collided with Rachel's. He smiled down at her with a look that warmed his blue eyes and, in the process, melted her insides.

"I'm glad you came."

So was she, until she remembered why.

Her humming endocrines cooled their jets. The smile in Jake's eyes would die an instant death if he knew the real reason she was here. Half wishing she'd never glanced at the bill he'd pulled out of his wallet, Rachel followed her aunt through the door he held open for them.

The raucous din inside the house matched the noise outside. Squeals, high-pitched shrieks, and the teeth-gritting wail of sirens almost drowned an exasperated parental command.

"Take those things outside!"

More shrieks followed the admonishment, accompanied by the bang of something hitting a wall. Seconds later, two pint-sized intergalactic warriors wielding noisy ray guns barreled around the corner and careened down the tiled hall.

"Watch it!"

With the agility of a man used to dodging cattle, Jake whipped past Alice. He scooped one warrior up under his arm and caught the other by the straps of her bunny-pink corduroy jumper a half second before she crashed into the walker.

"Got ya!" the towheaded girl shouted gleefully,

aiming her weapon at the squirming bundle under Jake's arm. Her neon yellow gun barrel spewed a shower of blue sparks. Electronic pops and whistles screeched from the handle.

"I gotted you first!" her adversary cried, wriggling into position to return fire. "You're dead, Kasey."

"Nossir! *You're* dead, 'n' smellier 'n a pile of cow poopy."

"Kasey Anne Henderson!"

The ominous exclamation silenced the ray guns instantly. A petite blonde in well-washed jeans and a moss-green sweater that matched her eyes swept around the corner. She grimaced apologetically at the three adults before addressing the older of the two combatants.

"Did I just hear you call your cousin cow poop?"

The curly-haired cherub assumed a look of wounded innocence. "I just said Matt *smelled* like it. 'N' he does! 'Specially when he goes potty in his pants like he did this afternoon."

The boy's face crumpled at the reminder. With the smug superiority of one who'd already graduated from training pants, the girl smirked at her vanquished opponent.

"That's okay, sport." Maneuvering the toddler up onto his shoulders, Jake soothed his injured pride. "Accidents like that happened to all cowboys in their younger days."

"Did I hear someone mention accidents?"

With a note of wry resignation in her voice, the boy's mother joined the group gathered in the tiled hall. Her dark hair cascaded in shimmering waves over the shoulders of a cobalt-blue sweatshirt that announced the 2001 Cannes International Film Festival.

"What kind of accidents are we talking about here?"

"Nothing worth repeating," Jake answered in an obvious attempt to mend the breach between cousins.

His answer raised skeptical brows, but the newcomer didn't press the issue. Smiling, she offered her hand to Alice and Rachel and started the introductions.

"I'm Sydney, Reece's other half."

"And I'm Molly," the blonde supplied, ruffling her daughter's curls. "The mother of Princess Leia here and the two you hear squalling in the other room. One twin can't hiccup unless the other announces it to the world at the top of her lungs."

So this was Sam's wife. With her tip-tilted nose, slender figure and laughing green eyes, Molly Henderson didn't give the impression of a harried mother of three small girls. In fact, Rachel thought

with only the tiniest trace of envy, she looked like
a woman who loved life and was well loved in return.

Cocking an ear toward the living room, Molly
issued another warning. "Oh-oh. Brace yourself.
Sounds like the girls are working up to full volume.
I hope Jake gave you and Alice some idea of what
you're getting into tonight."

"He did."

"We'll try to keep the noise down to a roar
but..."

"Gotcha!"

Molly rolled her eyes as her daughter fired off
another round. With a triumphant snicker, the girl
raced away. Matt instantly demanded to be put
down and gave chase the moment his feet touched
tile. His noisy ray gun filled the hall with a shower
of green and blue sparks.

"Go outside!" both mothers shouted in unison.

Shaking her head, Sydney gave up. "Why don't
Molly and I take Alice to the living room and get
her comfortable? The men are in the kitchen. Martina's off tonight, so they're cooking," she warned.
"I hope you like biscuits, beans and beef, all
smothered in barbecue sauce."

"Sounds good to me."

Actually, the combination smelled a lot better
than it sounded. Rachel's mouth started watering

the moment she stepped through the swinging door into the huge, eat-in kitchen that obviously constituted the main gathering spot of the house. And if sizzling beef and yeasty biscuits hadn't stirred her appetite, the three Hendersons ranged around the table would have done the trick.

Good Lord! She'd never encountered so much rugged masculinity aggregated in one spot. Sam had firmed up considerably since that long ago summer when he was more rangy muscle than meat. Rachel certainly didn't remember his T-shirt straining across bulging biceps. Or an upper chest like a tank. Reece and Marsh obviously kept in shape, as well.

Yet as good as the younger Hendersons looked individually and collectively, it was their older brother who set off seismic tremors under Rachel's skin when he took her arm to guide her through an obstacle course of high chairs, playpens and jumper swings. She was still experiencing the rippling aftershocks when Sam and the others caught sight of the newcomers.

A grin lit the youngest Henderson's face. "Hey, Rachel," he said, rising with the innate grace that must come with the genes. "It's been a while."

"That it has."

"I hope you've forgiven me for whatever I said or did on our last date that landed me on my butt."

"If you can't even remember what it was," she answered with a chuckle, "it doesn't need forgiving."

"Whew! I skated on that one. Do you remember Reece and Marsh?"

"I do now. You've all, ah, matured a bit."

"So have you," Reece replied with a grin. "Jake noticed it right away."

"Did he?"

Rachel flicked a quick glance at the man beside her and caught the tail end of the warning Jake flashed his brother. Without missing a beat, Reece directed the conversation into different channels.

"I was sorry to hear about Alice. Hope she's adjusting to her new hip joint."

"She's getting around a lot better than either I or the doctors expected her to."

The other brother—Marsh—gave Sam a good-natured shove between the shoulder blades. "Let's go say hello while Jake gets Rachel something cold to drink. Keep an eye on the beans," he ordered on the way out.

The three men trooped through the swinging door, letting it swoosh shut behind them. Mindful of their parting orders, Rachel slid her hand into an oven mitt and lifted the lid on a simmering bean pot. Steam bathed her face and had her scrunching her eyes against the heat.

"We've got beer, white wine and iced tea," Jake told her. "Or I can mix you something stronger to get you through until the terrible twosome you met in the hallway hit the hay."

"Iced tea is fine."

She stirred the beans with a long handled wooden spoon while Jake retrieved a glass from the cabinet.

How odd that she felt right at home here in the spacious, cluttered kitchen. Back in D.C., her work kept her so busy her kitchen rarely saw even weekend duty.

With a smile, she accepted the glass of sweetened tea he handed her. He was drinking the same thing, she saw, and remembered how he'd opted for a soft drink last night at the fair instead of joining her in a beer. She doubted if his abstinence stemmed from religious principles, given the fact that his brothers obviously enjoyed their icy brews.

She caught herself making a mental note of the fact that Jake Henderson didn't drink. Dammit, she hadn't even been in the house ten minutes and she was already compiling a mental profile of the man for Russ Taggart.

This was going to be a looooong evening, Rachel thought as she tipped her tall, dew-streaked glass to his.

Contrary to her expectations, the hours flew by. Dinner was a noisy affair, with banging spoons and as much food dropped onto the tiles as made it into the youngsters' mouths. Conversation ranged from Sam's job as commander of an air force test facility to Sydney's current chances for the independent film critics' award to the current bestseller about a serial killer with a taste for human organs that both Alice and Molly had read with ghoulish fascination.

The noise levels diminished exponentially when Kasey and Matt were fed, bathed, and carted off to bed. It decreased even further when the twins curled up like pretzels in the portable playpen that served as their crib.

Breathing collective sighs of relief, the adults settled into the comfortable sofas and chairs clustered in front of the living room's massive stone fireplace. With various extremities propped on handy footstools or coffee tables, they downed dark, rich coffee swizzled with chocolate-coated cinnamon sticks.

"This," Sydney announced with a purr of pleasure, "is the best part of my day."

"It is, huh?" Reece gave her a lazy grin. "Guess that means the honeymoon is finally over."

Wrinkling her nose, his wife declined to be drawn into that patch of quicksand. Instead, she asked Rachel about her job.

"Jake said you're with the National Transportation and Safety Board."

"That's right."

"What exactly do you do?"

"I'm a senior safety analyst. I run tests on the composites used to manufacture trains, planes, trucks and automobiles. Pretty routine stuff most of the time."

"Don't let her kid you." With a huff of pride, Alice touted her niece's accomplishments. "She's an expert in accident reconstruction. Rachel's analysis helped determine that inadequate reinforcement of a brake shoe lining led to a seventeen car pileup on the Pennsylvania Turnpike. Just last year she was tapped for the special task force investigating the crash of the jet that flew into the mountains about a hundred miles from here."

"I remember that!" Molly exclaimed. "It made all the headlines."

Rachel's muscles tensed. Her glance slid to Jake. If the DC-10 crash held any special significance for him, he didn't show it.

"Did the investigation board ever determine the cause of the accident?"

Rachel pulled her gaze back to Sam. All air force pilot now, he leaned forward, wrists hooked over his knees, a frown creasing his forehead.

"The findings are still under review." She tossed

the question back at Sam. "Military and civilian aviation organizations receive copies of preliminary accident reports. Did you see them?"

"Yes."

"What did it look like from your perspective?"

"Like a cargo hatch blew and the resulting drag threw the pilots into an emergency mode," he said flatly. "The blizzard finished them off. The only question is what caused the cargo hatch to blow."

Or who, Rachel thought with a quick swallow. Her eyes flicked back to Jake.

No! There was no way he could have been involved in a scheme that ultimately sent four people plunging to their deaths.

Her belief became conviction as the evening wore on and she gathered more information about the oldest Henderson brother. Careful listening and a few casual questions elicited the information that the drop in beef prices last year had hit Jake as hard as the other ranchers in the area. The difference, Rachel learned, was that his brothers all still owned shares in the Bar-H. The Hendersons pulled together, in good times and in bad. The infusions of cash into the Bar-H's operating account must have come from its co-owners, or from Jake's mother Jess, who still apparently took an active interest in the operation.

With a sinking feeling, she guessed that Taggart would no doubt widen his probe to include everyone associated with the Bar-H, Jess Henderson included. Rachel had certainly opened a Pandora's box, one that might never close again.

When she and Alice finally rose to leave, she'd carried out at least two of Taggart's instructions. She'd kept her eyes and ears open, and she'd learned as much as she could about Jake Henderson.

She didn't consciously attempt to carry out Russ's third order and try to get close to Jake. It just...sort of happened when Alice made a detour to the bathroom before setting out on the drive home.

Rachel and her host drifted outside to wait for Alice. The bawling calves had quieted, thank goodness. A million stars pinwheeled through the sky. The honeysuckle blossoms had folded their petals, but their fragrance perfumed the night.

Jake didn't intend to kiss her. That much Rachel deduced later, when she'd recovered her senses enough to reconstruct the sequence of events with the same analytical precision she employed at work. Nor did he intend to do more than pluck a twisting strand of honeysuckle, breathe in a delighted whiff and lift it for Jake to enjoy.

He brought his head down to take a sniff.

The hand she raised almost clipped him on the chin.

He caught her wrist with a loose hold, grinning as he dodged the blow.

Their eyes locked.

It was as simple as that. And as shattering. In that brief moment of contact, his grin faded. The fingers he'd wrapped around her wrist tightened.

Those damned chemical signals coursing through Rachel's system started flashing red alert again. She murmured something. Or maybe Jake did. She wasn't sure. Didn't care. Raising up on tiptoe, she met him halfway.

The kiss was cool at first touch, not much more than a slide of lips on lips, but heated up fast. Shifting, Jake fit his mouth over hers. His hands framed her face. Fingers callused by rope and wire brushed her cheeks.

With a little sidestep of her own, Rachel fit her body against his. Need spilled into her, fast and greedy. She slid her hands up his arms, and her screaming endocrines went berserk. Everything that was female in her responded to the feel of his corded biceps, his hard mouth, the faint scent of leather and clean, sharp wind that clung to his shirt.

Yet some faint corner of her mind shouted that this was more than just a mindless, hormonal response. That it was Jake who'd found her hair trigger.

And only Jake, dammit!

Chapter 5

"I don't like this."

Her mouth set in stubborn lines, Rachel scowled at the FBI operative seated across from her in the back booth of the Downtowner Café. The noontime noise of the popular eatery Aunt Alice had owned and operated for so many years provided a protective shield for their conversation. Waitresses sang their orders to the cook at the grill. Customers laughed and chattered. Heavy platters in bright fiesta colors clunked on the Formica-topped tables and counter.

The new owners had wisely retained Alice's menu and decor—a mix of utilitarian diner, garish tourist kitsch, and stunning black-and-white photos taken by a long-ago student at the University of Northern Arizona who'd worked part-time as a dishwasher. The photos captured the area's sky-scraping mountains, deep box canyons, windswept high deserts, and ancient Anasazi ruins in dramatic visual detail. A spectacular series shot from the bottom of the Grand Canyon filled one whole wall.

Rachel's favorites, though, had always been the portraits lined up like a gallery of movie stars above the pass-through to the grill. Miners with coal-blackened faces stared down through raccoon white eyes. Broad-cheeked Navajos looked out over the diners impassively. Helmeted loggers, National Park Service rangers in their Smoky-the-Bear hats, and leather-tough wranglers ranged beside them.

It was one of those wranglers who now drew her gaze. Big John Henderson's photo had graced the wall for as long as Rachel could remember. He must have been in his late twenties or early thirties at the time the picture was taken. A hired hand then, Aunt Alice had told Rachel. Saving his wages to buy the first few acres that would eventually grow into the Bar-H. Eyes narrowed against the sun, gloved hands absently looping a lariat, he gazed at something beyond the camera's range. Like his sons, he was all lean muscle and sun-weathered skin.

And like his sons, he'd become a respected member of the Flagstaff community. Dragging her gaze back to Taggart, Rachel repeated her objections to continuing the charade he was still insisting on.

"I've been out to the Bar-H twice now. Once for dinner, once to return the favor by delivering the pecan-raisin pies Aunt Alice baked for the family."

Even now, her stomach hollowed at the memory of the scene that had greeted her when she'd pulled up at the ranch house the second time. She'd spotted Jake and his brothers down at the corrals, working alongside the Bar-H hands as they wrestled vociferously protesting calves into the transport trucks lined up like silvery dominoes. They had to ship this batch off to the feeder lots in Kansas and Oklahoma to make room for the next, Jake had explained when he saw her car and took a breather. Swiping his sweat-sheened forehead with his arm, he'd helped her carry the box of pies into the house.

Rachel had given Taggart an expurgated account of their conversation when they'd huddled together at the kitchen table for a slice of the still-warm pastry. She saw no reason to include unnecessary details. Like the way her glance had slipped to the neck of Jake's work shirt, where he'd left the top two buttons undone. Or how her stomach had jumped when he leaned over to wipe a trace of gooey pie filling from the corner of her lower lip with a fingertip. Or her shivery delight when she thought he was going to kiss her again, and biting disappointment when he didn't.

Taggart was only interested in Jake's casual invitation for Rachel to join him and the crew when they rode up to Three Rock Canyon tomorrow to bring down the next batch of calves.

"You've got to go," the agent insisted for the third or fourth time. Shadows circled his eyes. He hadn't slept much since her call three days ago, Rachel guessed.

Neither had she.

"We've run every member of Henderson's family through the computers. I can't come up with any connection to the downed aircraft."

Frustration added a sharp edge to his voice…and to Rachel's when she leaned forward and shot back, "Maybe that's because there isn't a connection. Why don't you just *ask* Jake where he got the bill?"

Like a bulldog with a ham bone between his jaws, the FBI operative had crunched down hard and refused to let go. "I'm not ready to tip my hand yet. Give me another day, Rache. Go with him tomorrow to… Where was it? Hard Rock Canyon?"

"Three Rock Canyon."

Her fingers beat a fast tattoo on the Formica tabletop. Brow furrowed, she weighed her responsibilities as a former member of the task force against her increasing attraction to Jake Henderson. For the life of her, Rachel couldn't have said which swayed her decision.

"All right. But this is the last time, Russ. I don't like lying to him."

"You're not lying. You're just not telling him the whole truth."

Somehow Rachel didn't think Jake would appreciate the fine distinction.

He didn't, but Rachel had no inkling of how explosive his reaction would be when she showed up at the Bar-H at six-thirty the next morning wearing jeans, boots, a long-sleeved shirt, and a lightweight jacket as instructed.

It was still dark. And cold! Rachel's definition of lightweight differed considerably from Jake's, she discovered when she stepped out of her car. September had put a decided bite in the predawn air. Shivering in her red windbreaker with "NTSB" emblazoned in four-inch black letters across the back, she joined the group gathered around a cluster of pickups and long, ventilated stock trailers.

Jake met her with a steaming thermos. "You look like you need something to kick-start your engines."

"I do. Mornings aren't my best times. I only come awake after a direct infusion of caffeine."

Gratefully, she wrapped both hands around the mug he handed her. The first sip opened her eyes and closed her throat.

"That'll do it," she told him, choking down thick, sludgy liquid.

"Sorry. I should have warned you Shad brewed up this batch."

Bow-legged and stoop-shouldered, the Bar-H's foreman ambled over. "You maligning my java again?"

"It's long past maligning."

"I was roastin' coffee beans over an open fire long before you got throwed off your first horse, boy." With that masterful put-down, the foreman turned his back on his employer and gave Rachel a thorough once-over. "So you're the one I've been hearin' about. Alice's niece, are you?"

"Yes."

"I'm Shadrach McCoy. Book of Daniel, chapter one, verse three."

"You must get asked about your name often," Rachel commented with a smile.

"Often enough." He rocked back on his heels, his face all leathery wrinkles and fuzzy whiskers under the brim of his battered felt cowboy hat.

"Good thing, you comin' out to look after your aunt, missy."

"She and Uncle Cal have always been kind to me. I'm just returning the favor."

"Good thing, anyway."

With a tip of his hat, he sauntered away. Rachel smiled after him. He was one of the old breed, she guessed. More at home on a horse than in a pickup.

"Has he been at the Bar-H long?"

"Since before I was born. Shad and my father cowboyed together in their younger days. Rode the rodeo circuit together, too, before Big John decided to invest his winnings in a few acres of Arizona scrub. He'd barely gotten the Bar-H going when Shad came to work alongside him one summer. The ornery old coot's been here ever since."

Rachel wasn't fooled for a moment. Jake's gruff description didn't disguise his affection for the bandy-legged foreman. Whatever else he'd done in his colorful past, Shad McCoy had certainly earned the Hendersons' respect.

"All right, boys and girls," McCoy called out in his tobacco-roughened voice. "Saddle up. Let's get this here circus on the road."

Circus pretty well described the bustle of activity that followed. Jake, his brothers and the other hands finished loading the horse trailers. That done, they tossed saddles, blankets and bridles into pickup beds, then checked the hitches on the cattle transports.

Lauren and Sydney strolled down from the house, laden with more thermoses. Molly, Rachel learned, had left her girls in the care of Jake's housekeeper and planned to accompany Sam in the twin-engine Cessna airplane parked at the end of the grassy airstrip behind the barns. When the cavalcade was ready to roll, Sam and his wife climbed into the cockpit and began the preflight warm-up. Within moments, the whine of an engine revving up split the morning quiet.

"They'll scout the canyons from the sky," Jake shouted above the engines. "Radio in the location of strays. Ready?"

Nodding, Rachel climbed into the lead pickup. The driver's side door slammed a moment later, closing her inside the dark, single-seat cab with Jake. He twisted the ignition key and gunned the powerful engine. With the rest of the pickups and trailers strung out behind them, they rattled across the cattle guard and aimed straight at the slanting rays painting the eastern sky a bright gold-pink.

"We brought the herd down to an accessible meadow last week, but some will have strayed off into the trees or adjoining canyons. We'll have to ride in after them. You can stay at the base camp if you don't feel up to two or three hours in the saddle."

"I can manage a couple of hours...I think."

The dubious reply earned her a chuckle. "We always pack a good supply of liniment."

"Will you rub down the parts I can't reach?"

The moment the flippant response was out, Rachel wished it back. She hadn't thought beyond a glib retort, certainly hadn't intended any sexual connotation. Yet the idea of Jake's hands gliding over her body started an instantaneous chain reaction. Her nerve endings sizzled. Heat jumped along her veins. She squirmed in her seat, annoyed, irritated, and more than a little dismayed by the way her inner thermostat clicked up several degrees every time she was around the man.

Jake felt it, too. The unexpected spark. The sudden surge of warmth. Rachel saw it in the way his grip tightened on the steering wheel. Heard it in the silence that settled over the cab, displacing their easy camaraderie. She was searching for a way to recover when he cleared his throat.

"Look, Rachel... About that kiss the other night. I need to explain."

She tried to recapture the nonchalance of a moment ago with an airy grin. "It was pretty self-explanatory to me."

"You don't understand." He stared out the windshield, negotiating the dirt road with careful precision. "Ellen and I were married for ten years. We went together for almost six years before that. I can't... I don't..."

A muscle jumped in the side of his jaw. The shadowy movement started a little ache just under Rachel's ribs. Reaching across the console, she laid a hand on his sleeve of his flannel-lined denim jacket.

"It was just a kiss."

When his jaw flexed again, her fingers curled into the soft fabric. "Jake..."

"I want more."

"What?"

"I want more than a kiss from you, Rachel." Dragging his eyes from the road ahead, he nailed her to her seat. "It started at the fair, when we danced. Came hammering home last night, when I wiped that bit of pie from your mouth. I wanted to kiss you again."

Since he made the confession with all the enthusiasm of a man about to have his wisdom teeth yanked without the benefit of anesthetic, Rachel didn't feel particularly flattered. Turned on, yes. Flattered, no.

"You don't sound very happy about the situation."

"I'm not."

His blunt reply destroyed any inclination she might have had to tell him she'd indulged in some wanting of her own.

"If I bother you so much, why did you invite me to come along today?"

"Because you bother me so much."

"Oh, that makes a lot of sense!"

"I know." Frustration laced his voice. He shoved a hand through his hair, started again. "I'm handling this all wrong. It's been a long time since I had to apologize for acting like a pimply teenager with hyperactive glands."

"Is that what this is supposed to be? An apology?"

"I'm just trying to tell you that you don't have to worry about that kiss the other night," he ground out. "It won't happen again."

The flat assertion raised a nasty little itch in Rachel. She had the craziest urge to take the initiative and prove just how wrong he could be. Pride kept her from scratching the itch, however.

Pride and common sense.

Frowning, she flopped back against the seat. The dawn that streaked the sky with such glorious swirls of red and gold and pink suddenly seemed like a giant mirror, reflecting her own swirling confusion. She had to admit her motivation for joining Jake on this morning's expedition was as convoluted as his apparently was for inviting her.

Taggart had pushed her, sure, but she'd been pushed before. She hadn't reached her position as a senior analyst at the NTSB without learning how to deal with the pressure that came at her from all sides. When she released her findings in a high-profile or controversial accident investigation, that pressure tripled in intensity. She couldn't count the number of times she'd stood toe to toe with angry officials from the Airline Pilots Association, the Railroaders Association, or the International Truckers Union, not to mention her peers within the Department of Commerce itself.

No, Taggart wasn't the reason she was jouncing along a dirt road in the chilly dawn. Only a foot or two of airspace separated her from the real reason.

She slanted Jake another look, chewing over his words. He wanted her, but he wasn't going to do anything about it.

Well, hell.

He'd been right to get it out in the open, Jake decided as the pickup jolted down the dirt track. Right to let Rachel know he recognized that he'd been putting out dangerously mixed signals.

He'd thought it through, wrestled hard with the knowledge that she stirred responses in him he didn't want to feel. Wasn't ready to feel. He'd acknowledged that sobering fact last night, right after he'd issued the crazy invitation for her to ride out with him this morning.

He hadn't intended to invite her, any more than he'd intended to kiss her the other night on the

porch. Or let his finger graze her mouth when he'd
removed that morsel of pie. Just thinking about her
red, luscious mouth had sent Jake to bed hard and
aching. Again! He'd rolled out of bed this morning
determined to set things square between them.

Well, he'd pretty well bungled the matter, but at
least he'd said what needed saying. He'd loved Ellen. He would always love Ellen. Whatever itchy
feelings Rachel Quinn raised under his skin
couldn't touch the place in his heart his wife would
always hold. Rachel needed to know that, right up
front, just as Jake had needed to tell her the way
things were. His sense of fairness wouldn't allow
him to take this crazy attraction between them any
further. Or let her think he was offering more than
he could deliver.

Now that he'd said his piece, maybe he could put
that blasted kiss out of his head and concentrate on
the tasks at hand…the first being to get them to the
meadow that would serve as their base camp without busting an axle.

Hands tight on the wheel, Jake steered the pickup
along the rutted road that wound up into the Coconino National Forest. Like most of the big ranchers in the area, he leased grazing rights on the federal preserves that covered a good chunk of
northern Arizona.

This particular preserve consisted of almost two
million acres containing everything from semiarid

desert to ponderosa pine forests to alpine tundra. Elevations ranged from two thousand feet above sea level at some of the canyon bottoms to more than twelve thousand feet at the top of the San Francisco Peaks. It was a tough land, an unforgiving land to those whose lives were affected by the searing droughts, the wild gales, the fierce snowstorms that often ravaged the area. To someone born and bred in the shadow of those jagged peaks, though, it was as close to heaven as a man was likely to get while he still drew breath.

With each hairpin turn in the road, stubby live oak and piñon gave way to fir and pine. Increasingly, the air took on a sharp bite of resin flavored with the damp, earthy odor of rotting logs. The verdant richness filled Jake's lungs when at last he pulled the pickup off the road into a broad, flat meadow and climbed out.

Squinting in the bright morning sunshine, he spotted a dozen or so head of Brangus and black Angus at the far end of the meadow. The rest of the herd had drifted into the tree-lined slopes on either side of the valley.

Jake and his hands had brought this bunch down from the high summer pastures a week ago and sorted out the bull calves and heifers he wanted to keep for breeding stock. Now came the real work. He was pulling on his worn leather gloves when Shad descended from the second pickup.

"All right, boys and girls," the foreman croaked. "Time to earn your keep."

Idly, Jake wondered how many times he'd heard Shad McCoy issue that same gruff announcement. A hundred times at least.

Gray-haired, stoop-shouldered, and as stubborn as a bent nail, the old man could have retired years ago. He certainly possessed the financial resources to kick back, prop his heels on a porch rail and never wrestle another bawling calf into a chute again. Both Big John and Jake, when he took over management of the Bar-H, made it a practice to match the contributions their employees made to retirement funds.

Shad was far more than an employee, however. And Jake was damned if he was going to be the one to suggest retirement to the man who'd wheezed with laughter every time one of the Henderson boys had parted company with a horse, then dusted them off and put them right back in the saddle.

Shad ambled over. His rheumy eyes flicked an assessing glance over Rachel as she leaned against the front of the pickup, her hands pushed into her jacket pockets.

"I've got an extra pair of gloves in my truck if you've a mind to help out."

"That's why I'm here."

"Good enough. You come with me, missy, and I'll show you what to do."

Rachel was soon hard at work helping unload and water the horses while Jake, his brothers and their hands muscled the portable corrals out of the stock trailers and into place. They'd all shed their jackets and rolled up their sleeves by the time the last section clanked into place.

Rachel had worked up a sweat, too, Jake saw. Perspiration shone on her nose and cheeks when she drifted over to join him beside the corral.

"What do we do now?" Shading her eyes, she surveyed the herd at the far end of the meadow. "Ride down and shoo them back this way?"

He hid a smile at her description of the dusty, frustrating chore of pushing a bunch of cows in a direction they didn't particularly want to go.

"The easiest way to handle cattle is to make them come to you. We'll try this first."

Wedging a shoulder inside a pickup's open window, he leaned on the horn. A series of shrill blasts rolled down the meadow. Echoes bounced back from the slopes on either side.

It only took one cow to get the herd moving. A beefy black Angus lifted her head, swung it to identify the source of the noise and started for the trucks. Her calf trotted along behind her. The rest of the herd soon followed in their wake.

"That's it?" Rachel demanded incredulously. "You just toot the horn and they come?"

"Those that can hear it. We'll have to mount up and search out the rest."

Obviously, the technique he'd described didn't jibe with Hollywood's version of a cattle drive. Rachel looked both amused and disappointed.

"You just toot the horn?" she repeated with a shake of her head.

Grinning, Jake confessed the secret of modern-day ranching. "We always carry sorghum molasses feed cakes when we come up to check stock. They've learned that the sound of the horn means a treat."

"You know you're destroying all my illusions about you rough, tough cowboys, don't you?"

His grin took a wry tilt. "Yeah. I know."

Jake restored at least some of her faith in cowboys later that afternoon, when they went in search of the cows Sam had spotted in an aerial sweep of a small, rocky canyon.

In the process, however, he shattered his own illusion that he could keep his hands off Rachel Quinn.

Chapter 6

They found the three cows strung out along a narrow canyon cut by a deep gully. Two stood nursing their offspring. The third peered down into the gully and mooed plaintively to her bawling calf. The knob-kneed black Angus had managed to slide down into the gulch and now couldn't climb back up. His heartrending cries rode on the wind that whistled along the pine-studded canyon walls.

"Poor baby," Rachel murmured, moved by his plight.

Jake wasn't quite as sympathetic. With a few choice words about damn fool cattle that don't have sense enough to stick to grassy meadows, he swung off his horse and untied the lariat lashed to the saddle.

Rachel dismounted as well, fascinated by his smooth coordination as he snaked out the rope. He looped one end around the saddle horn, then draped the remaining length over a tall pine that seemed to jut out from solid rock. The scientist in Rachel appreciated his use of the simple laws of physics. The tree trunk would act as a fulcrum, she saw at once, and prevent the sharp rocks at the edge of the gully from sawing into the rope. His horse would provide the force required to pull the calf up the slope.

The big bay gelding stood patiently, tail swishing. Obviously, both man and horse had done this drill before. Nevertheless, Rachel felt compelled to offer her less than expert assistance.

"Do you need me to hold his reins? Back him up when it's time to haul up the calf or something?"

"Hammer here knows what to do, don't you boy?"

His affectionate slap raised puffs of dust from his mount's neck. Hammer nickered and tossed his head.

"Just keep back from the edge," Jake cautioned, wrapping the rope around his waist a couple of times. "The dirt might crumble under your boots."

Mindful of his warning, she watched the proceedings from a safe distance. Hammer, she discovered, did indeed know just what to do. Bracing his forelegs, he stood unmoving while Jake worked his way down the slope hand over hand. He reached the bottom a few moments later and unwound the rope.

Now that rescue was at hand, the ungrateful calf didn't appear to want it. Skittish and bleating more loudly than ever, it backed up the narrow gulch. Jake followed, snaking out a loop in the stiff hemp. A moment later, the lasso sailed through the air and settled around the calf's neck. A quick tug tightened the noose.

Just like in the movies, Rachel thought in satisfaction. Her faith in cowboys restored, she watched as Jake took up the slack and gave a piercing whistle. Hammer began to back up slowly, dragging the calf with him. Bucking and twisting at the end of his tether, the animal started up the slope. His hooves scrabbled for purchase on the loose rocks. His vociferous protests reverberated through the canyon and made Rachel wince in silent sympathy.

Unfortunately, the pathetic cries also agitated his worried mama. Bawling in response to her calf's cries, she nosed right to the brink of the ledge. Her front hooves sent a shower of dirt and loose rocks rattling down the slope. Fearing she might go over

the side and land on top of her calf or Jake or both,
Rachel flapped her arms.

"Get back! Shoo!"

She should have realized a mama in the throes
of panic for her baby wouldn't be shooed. Instead
of retreating, the beefy animal swung toward the
new threat. Emitting something between a moo and
a growl, she lowered her head and charged.

"Hey!"

Rachel didn't have time to think, didn't have
time for anything except immediate evasive action.
The rope was stretched taut at the small of her back,
blocking retreat. Hammer stood braced on his forelegs at her immediate right. That left only the gully
on the left. With a warning yelp to Jake, she
plunged over the edge.

Her feet went out from under her halfway down
the steep slope. She landed on her bottom and
bounced the rest of the way, passing the calf on his
journey up. She had a fleeting impression of a wet
black nose and startled brown eyes mere seconds
before an iron band clamped around her flailing
arm. Jake jerked her to a halt, digging in his boot
heels to steady himself against the pull of her
weight.

"Hang on!"

As if she could do anything else with him man-
acling her wrist! Dangling by one arm, Rachel

flopped like a landed trout. Rocks loosened by her wild slide and the hooves of the calf now scrambling the last few feet to his mama tumbled down around her head.

She flung up her free arm to protect herself... or tried to. Her elbow collided with a hard chest as Jake threw himself down to shield her. His weight landed full on top of her. Her breath left with a whoosh. Pinned between the unyielding slope and Jake's solid, equally unyielding mass, Rachel sucked in swift, shallow gulps of air.

Those quick little gasps proved a serious mistake. Every rise of her breasts mashed them against Jake's chest. Every panting breath brought his scent with it. Leather and male, horse and dust. The combination was so rich, so heady that she was still gasping when he eased the bulk of his weight from her prone body.

Worry roughened his voice. His blue eyes raked her face. "Are you all right?"

"I think so."

With their legs tangled and her wrist still caught in his grip, she tried an experimental wiggle. The tentative movement produced no sharp pains or serious aches. Just a sudden, intense sensation.

Belatedly, Rachel discovered that Jake had wedged a knee between her legs to anchor himself in place. His thigh now rode as hard as a fence pole

against the inner seam of her jeans. Gulping down
another quick rush of air, she tried for cheery and
nonchalant.

"I don't think anything's broken except my dig-
nity."

Afterward, she could never satisfactorily analyze
just what she'd expected from Jake at that point. A
disgusted reminder that he'd warned her to stand
back from the edge, maybe. At the very least, a
demand to know why the hell she'd come slithering
down the slope on her backside. What she didn't
expect was the laughter that slid into his eyes.

"After a wild ride like that one, you're going to
need that liniment for sure," he said.

This time, she managed to bite back the invitation for him to rub it on. But she couldn't hold back
her little shiver of delight when he lifted a hand and
brushed her tangled hair away from her cheek. His
touch was so tender, yet so tantalizing that the air
she'd managed to pull into her lungs whooshed
right out again.

"Jake…"

At her husky murmur, regret replaced laughter
she'd glimpsed in his eyes a second before. Rachel
could feel his withdrawal even before he eased his
body away from hers.

"Come on, I'll help you up."

"I want you, too."

Her breathless admission froze him in place. His gaze sliced down to hers. Rachel saw a frown form and recklessly plunged ahead. He might try to suppress the sparks that flew every time they got within twenty feet of each other, but there was no way she could ignore the heat that sizzled just under her skin whenever and wherever he touched her.

"I just want to keep things clear between us," she said gruffly.

As clear as they could be between a member of an interagency task force and a possible suspect.

Like a pesky little gnat that wouldn't go away her conscience buzzed at her. She should tell him about Russ Taggart. She should let Jake know that he wasn't the only one hauling around a mixed bag of emotions about this crazy attraction between them. She'd given Russ enough time to run his computer queries and background checks. She owed Jake the truth.

She came within a breath of confessing, was searching for just the right way to bring the investigation out in the open, when other matters took priority. Most notably, Jake's reaction to her blunt admission that she wanted him. An ache started in the middle of Rachel's chest as she watched his frown fade and his expression go distant with memories of another time, another woman.

"I know," she whispered, reaching up to stroke

his bristly cheek. "You loved Ellen. You still love her."

His silence thundered in her ears. She might have lost her nerve at that point if he hadn't blinked. His blue eyes shifted, focused once again on her. The painful past still lingered in their depths, but Rachel saw her own image reflected there as well.

"You and I aren't to the point of loving yet," she said slowly. "We might never be. But I'm willing to see where this leads if you are."

When he didn't answer, Rachel slid her hand from his cheek and threaded it through the damp, springy hair at his nape. Soft as a whisper, gentle as the breeze that sighed through the pines, she fit her mouth to his.

He'd warned her. The thought ricocheted through Jake's head as he drank in her taste. He'd told her flat out that he wanted her, that she stirred needs he was trying his damnedest to keep under control. Too late he realized his warning should have been directed at himself and not her.

One touch, and he wanted more. One taste, and heat exploded in his veins. He fought the sensations. Refused to acknowledge his need until Rachel's mouth opened under his.

Her tongue offered a pleasure he'd denied for so long. Too long, he thought on a rush of hunger. With a swift pull, Jake scooted her back under him, positioned her so that her body fused with his at a dozen different pleasure points. Angling his head, he deepened the kiss.

After the first, muffled gasp, Rachel answered with a flaring hunger that fed his. Legs tangling, lips warm and pliant, she jerked loose the wrist he'd forgotten he still held and wrapped both arms around his neck. A distant corner of Jake's mind registered the dust still floating in the air around them. Spared a fleeting thought for the horses waiting patiently above. Worried that he was too heavy for her.

If he was, she didn't seem to mind. Her tongue played with his, teasing, taunting. Their teeth clicked, scraped. Desire coiled hot and urgent in Jake's gut with each bump of their noses and chins, each twist of her hips under his. Rock hard and aching, he raised his knee to ease the pressure of his too-tight jeans.

Or tried to. It was the same knee he'd wedged between Rachel's thighs to keep her from sliding the rest of the way down the gully. The movement, slight as it was, unintentionally increased the pressure on her mound and generated an instantaneous reaction. She arched her head, breaking the kiss. Red rushed into her cheeks. She let out a low, ragged hiss that could have been a sigh or a moan, and Jake's control slipped its last restraints.

He forgot the fact she'd just bumped down a rocky slope on her bottom, no doubt collecting a few bruises along the way. Forgot his determination to put her out of his head and out of his dreams. Forgot that she wasn't Ellen.

It was Rachel who fanned this heat in his belly. Rachel who writhed under him, her mouth as greedy as his. Rachel who yanked his shirttails out of his jeans with the same ferocity he attacked her jacket. The red NTSB windbreaker had twisted under her. Grunting with a combination of frustration and urgency, Jake snaked an arm around the small of her back and lifted her. He had to tug at the slippery material twice before he could get the zipper within reach.

With the windbreaker out of the way, he made short work of her knit top. A single glance at the stiff, dusky nipple pushing against the cream-colored bra told him she'd reached the same flash point he had.

The visible evidence of her excitement almost pushed Jake over the edge. He came within a half a breath of ripping off that scrap of lace, taking her tender flesh in his mouth, tormenting her with his teeth and tongue.

He ached for her. Wanted her more than he'd imagined he could want any woman again in this lifetime. But he wasn't going to yank down her jeans and mount her like a stallion after a mare in heat. She deserved better. She deserved more.

"Rachel."

Smoothing back her tangled hair, he willed his hand to a gentleness he was far from feeling.

"Sweetheart."

She blinked, her body still trembling with eagerness under his. A question formed in her brown-green eyes as she took in his expression. Jake answered it with an honesty that almost ripped him apart.

"I think we should see where this leads, too."

The hoarse admission cost him more than he'd anticipated. Memories swirled. Pain pulled at his heart. Ruthlessly, he ignored both.

"But not here," he said gruffly. "Not like this. I didn't anticipate... I wasn't planning..."

He gave a quick shake of his head, disgusted with his fumbling attempt to explain.

"I don't have anything to protect you."

It took a moment for Rachel's still reeling senses to grasp his meaning. Surprise replaced the chill of his withdrawal, bringing with it a rush of warmth.

She'd always assumed responsibility for her own protection. She was too intelligent to leave something so important to chance. And the men she'd dated, including the smooth, handsome congressional staffer she'd been seeing for almost a year, had always expected her to take care of things.

That Jake would put her welfare before the hunger she'd felt in his hard mouth and rough hands made the other men she'd known seem shallow and self-serving by contrast. It also opened a little door in Rachel's heart she suspected would never quite close.

In that moment, she said a swift, silent goodbye to Dale, who'd been pushing for the commitment Rachel wasn't ready for. She'd call him, she swore. Tonight. Tell him the instincts that had held her back, the doubts she'd hoped to sort through during her visit to Arizona, had finally crystallized. She knew now that they weren't right for each other, knew why the future she'd tried to envision with him had never jelled.

She'd been searching for Jake. Wanting him. Waiting for him.

Now that she'd found him, she decided wryly, she could wait a little longer. Jake was right. This wasn't the time or the place. Sam and his wife might fly overhead at any moment. The cows staring down at them from the ledge were too interested an audience. Besides, there was a jagged rock digging a permanent hole in her hip.

"We'll try this again sometime soon," she murmured, brushing her mouth across his. "With no rocks or bawling calves to distract us."

"Very soon."

The soft promise sent a thrill down her spine, as did Jake's strength as he helped her up the slope. Her hand clasped tight in his, Rachel clambered back onto the ledge.

By the time they arrived back at the valley, she ached in every part of her body. The combination of several hours in a saddle and her precipitous slide down a rocky canyon wall had left her legs so rubbery she could barely climb into the pickup for the drive home.

Sliding a hand under her arm, Jake helped her into the cab. The small but intimate courtesy didn't go unnoticed by his brothers or sisters-in-law. Rachel caught their swift exchange of looks, just as she'd picked up on the speculative glances the rest of the Henderson clan had aimed their way when she and Jake had brought in the stray cows and their calves.

She'd done her best to shake the dust and dirt from her clothes and hair before they left the canyon, but a single peek in the pickup's visor mirror illustrated the futility of her efforts. Makeup-less, tangle-haired, her lips red and swollen from Jake's kisses, Rachel gave up worrying about appearances during the long ride back to the Bar-H.

The silence that settled in the cab differed considerably from the charged tension that had gripped her and Jake during the drive out. He still had doubts. Still grappled with his guilt and memories of Ellen. Rachel accepted that, even as she acknowledged that her own doubts had disappeared. Anticipation hummed in her veins, along with a sense of rightness she'd never experienced before. The future hovered before her, lit with the same shimmering, seductive glow the colored lights had cast that night at the fair.

She was still basking in the glow when they arrived at the ranch with the cavalcade of trucks and stock trailers strung out behind them. Rachel slid out of the pickup and grabbed for the frame. She clung to it for support while her legs wobbled like half-set Jell-O.

Frowning, Jake came around the front of the pickup. "You okay?"

She gave him the same answer she had after her precipitous descent into the gully. "I think so."

"You're too shaky to walk. Why don't I carry you into the house? You could put your feet up and rest while we finish out here."

As delightful as that sounded, Rachel shook her head. "And admit that I'm a wimp in front of your brothers and the rest of the crew? No way. Just give me a minute or two. I'll be all right.''

A smile edged its way through his concern. ''I can think of a lot of ways to describe you, Ms. Quinn. Wimp isn't one of them.''

That perked her up considerably. With an answering grin, she waggled her brows and was about to inquire just what adjectives he'd use when a short, stocky figure strode around the side of the house.

The silly grin froze on Rachel's face. Her stomach plummeted halfway to her boots. Russ Taggart's expression as he raked a hard glance over his only lead in a year-long investigation sent it plunging the rest of the way.

''Mr. Henderson?''

Jake's gaze drifted over the newcomer's jeans, white cotton shirt and lightweight sports coat. ''Yes.''

Taggart slipped a hand inside his jacket and extracted a black leather case. With a quick twist of his wrist, he flipped it open. His nickel-plated badge gleamed dully in the afternoon sunshine.

''I'm Russell Taggart, FBI Special Agent in Charge.''

''In charge of what?''

With a cool, assessing glance, Taggart tucked the ID case back into his pocket. ''Among other things,

I'm heading the investigation into the crash of a chartered DC-10 that went down in the mountains north of here last year.''

Frowning, Jake looked to Rachel. He was remembering their conversation the other night, she guessed. Recalling how Aunt Alice had bragged about her niece's role in this very investigation.

''We need to talk to you, Mr. Henderson.''

Jake's glance cut back to the FBI agent. ''What about?''

''About the fifty-dollar bill you passed at the fair a few nights ago. We have reason to think it came from a DC-10 that crashed last year. We've been trying to ascertain just how the bill came into your possession ever since Ms. Quinn reported seeing you take it out of your wallet.''

Chapter 7

Rachel had faced down some formidable opponents in her career. Her analyses and findings had put her on the firing line often enough that she'd learned to take angry denials and countercharges with an impersonal objectivity.

But there was nothing impersonal about her reaction to the sudden narrowing of Jake's eyes. Her stomach churning, she stiffened against the anger that slowly reddened the skin of his cheeks.

"You reported me to the FBI?"

"Yes."

"The same night we met at the fair?"

"Yes."

His fury cut loose, stinging her like the steel-tipped prongs of a bullwhip. Even as he lashed into her, Rachel could see he was as disgusted with himself as he was with her.

"Dammit! I've tied myself up in knots over you these past few days. Made a total ass of myself. And all the while you were waiting for your friend here to... How did he put it? *Ascertain* just how that fifty came into my possession?"

She tied herself up in as many knots as he had, but Rachel could see he wasn't ready to hear that.

"Yes."

Jake moved toward her then. Only a few inches. Just enough to make her lift her chin and prompt Taggart to step into the breach. His voice bristling with authority, the agent attempted to gain control of the situation.

"Ms. Quinn was part of the initial accident investigation team. Of course she would report her sighting of that bill, just as she agreed to maintain personal contact with you while we ran our checks."

Jake hooked a sardonic brow. "Is that what they're calling it these days?"

The scorn in his voice could have peeled the bark off a ponderosa pine. Rachel certainly felt as though she'd lost a layer or two of skin.

"Jake..."

"I'll admit you had me fooled during the little scene in the canyon this afternoon. Just how much *personal contact* were you prepared to maintain during the course of your investigation, Ms. Quinn?"

As angry now as he was, Rachel fired back. "What happened in the canyon this afternoon had nothing to do with that blasted fifty-dollar bill. It had nothing to do with anything except you and me."

"Yeah, right."

"Dammit, Jake, I wasn't stringing you along this afternoon. I..."

"Got a problem here, big brother?"

Her fists clenching, Rachel bit back her hot denials as Reece and Marsh appeared and ranged themselves on either side of their sibling.

"Apparently I do," Jake answered through tight clenched teeth.

Sydney and Lauren drifted up to join their husbands, as did Shad McCoy and a few of the hands. Together, they formed an impenetrable phalanx.

"This is Special Agent Russell Taggart," Jake bit out. "He's with the FBI. He and Miss Quinn seem to think I've been passing stolen money."

"What?"

Shock, surprise and disbelief chased across the others' faces.

"Not stolen," Taggart corrected. "At this point, it's still classified as missing."

There was an almost imperceptible ripple of movement among the Hendersons. Shoulders squared. Jaws tightened. When Rachel caught Reece's hard look, she could have sworn she heard a door slam.

Suddenly, she was an outsider. Not just an outsider. An enemy, or at least a threat.

Reece wasn't the only one who put her on the other side of the threshold. Marsh shot her a narrow-eyed glance as he wrapped the mantle of his own law enforcement background around his brother like a shield.

"You carrying some identification on you, Taggart?"

The cold demand raised spots of color in the FBI operative's cheeks. Once more, he dug in his pocket for his ID case.

Marsh took his time examining his credentials. Far more time than Jake had. The DEA agent was making a statement, Rachel realized. Letting Taggart know that he wasn't impressed or intimidated. That message became crystal clear when he held on to the leather case instead of tossing it back to Taggart.

"You don't mind if I verify you're who you say you are?"

"No."

"Good. Let's go inside and I'll make a few calls."

Rachel didn't quite understand how the power had shifted so subtly or so swiftly, but shift it had. The Hendersons filed into the house, leaving her and Russ to follow on their own.

Feeling more wretched by the moment, she delayed Taggart with a hand on his arm. "What's going on? Why did you show up without any warning and cut the ground out from under my feet?"

"You're the one who insisted on confronting Henderson directly, remember?"

"Not in front of his entire family and a half dozen of his ranch hands!"

"It's done."

Taggart shrugged off her hand and headed for the front steps. Furious that he'd set her up like this, Rachel swooped around him and planted herself square in his path.

"Not so fast, Russ. I'm telling you here and now that you'd better not make unilateral decisions like this one. Not if you want my cooperation now or any time in the immediate future. Now give! What changed? Why are you here?"

Obviously annoyed at being taken to task, the agent shoved a hand through his buzz cut fair hair. "I ran out of options, okay? None of the queries or background checks I ran on Henderson and his family turned up any connection to the bill. Neither did my network of external resources.''

''So you decided it was time to go directly to the source,'' Rachel finished, still tight with anger. ''I'll say it one more time, Russ. No more decisions on your own if you want my help.''

Anger flashed in his dark eyes. He controlled it with a visible effort.

''I'll consult with you on any decisions that involve you. Now can we get in there and hear what Henderson has to say about the damned bill?''

''I got it from Grizzly.''

Pointedly, Jake ignored the woman across the living room from him as he answered Taggart's question.

She stood with her arms folded across her chest. Her hair was still windblown and wild from the drive home, her lips bare of any hint of color. The knowledge that he'd kissed it away only an hour ago put a kink in Jake's gut that refused to go away.

He'd deal later with his stupidity in mistaking a hard case of the hots for something else entirely, he told himself grimly. Right now Russell Taggart demanded his full attention.

The agent moved in short, jerky paces between the bookcase and the fireplace, obviously feeling too restless or too unwelcome to sit. Jake supposed he couldn't blame the man. With seven hostile Hendersons occupying strategic positions around the living room, the FBI operative probably felt he needed to remain a moving target.

"Grizzly?" Taggart repeated. "Are we talking a man or a bear here?"

"A man."

The clipped response tightened his mouth. He shot Jake a hard look and got one back in return. Marsh's verification of the agent's credentials hadn't tempered Jake's instinctive dislike. He didn't appreciate being played for a fool any more than the next man.

Still, from the sparse details Taggart had shared before plunging into his questions, it appeared the bill Jake had passed at the fair could have some connection to a downed aircraft. He felt a reluctant obligation to provide whatever information he could.

"Grizzly's real name is Isaac McCoy. He's a distant cousin of our foreman. He got his nickname from the cub he took in and raised some years ago."

"And this Grizzly guy passed you the fifty?"

"Yes."

"Did he say where he got it?"

"No."

The two men locked eyes. Taggart did a silent ten count. "Would you get him in here so I can ask?"

"No."

The agent's face purpled. Jake allowed himself a brief stab of satisfaction before relenting.

"He's a recluse. An eccentric recluse."

Actually, all five Henderson brothers had privately agreed when they were growing up that Grizzly McCoy was crazy as a loon. The old man would scare the pants off them when he'd appear suddenly at the Bar-H in search of his cousin, one eye wide and unfocused, the other darting wildly from side to side. If he'd bathed any time in the past half century, he sure didn't smell like it. His long, scraggly beard carried more fleas than a barn cat.

He'd taken a bullet through the brain box in Korea, Shad had explained in his laconic way. Never was quite right after that.

He had a way with wild creatures, though, and Shad feared he'd go completely off the deep end if locked away, like some veterans coordinator up in Colorado had recommended. Big John had offered him work at the Bar-H, but Isaac had preferred the isolation of the mountains. After Big John and Shad had fixed up an old, deserted line shack for him, the man had melted into the pine-shrouded canyons.

As far as Jake knew, the cub he'd rescued and raised by hand was his only companion.

"He lives in an abandoned Bar-H line shack up in the mountains. Every six months or so, he comes down to collect his pension checks, stock up on supplies and hand me the rent he insists on paying. Last time, he paid with three crisp, new fifty-dollar bills. I thought he got them at the bank when he cashed his checks."

"When was that?" Taggart asked sharply.

"Two, three weeks ago."

"Do you have the other bills?"

"They're in the cash box in my office."

"May I see them?"

With a curt nod, Jake left the room. He returned a few moments later with the notes. Taggart almost snatched them out of his hand. Fierce satisfaction flared in his dark eyes.

"They're from the same serial number sequence," he told Rachel.

Acutely aware that Jake had ignored her from the moment she'd walked into the room, she took the notes Taggart held out. The paper felt stiff and sticky, the way new bills always did. Slowly, she rubbed them between her fingers. She'd learned enough during her months on the task force to know paper money was produced using a method called intaglio printing. The paper was forced at high speeds through plates crafted by skilled artists, engravers and printers. Because the plates were three dimensional, one side of new bills always feels slightly raised, while the reverse feels a little indented.

The difference was so slight most people never noticed it. Unless she'd known what to feel for, Rachel wouldn't have noticed it, either. She rubbed the crisp new fifty between her fingers and blew out a long breath. Wherever this Grizzly McCoy had found these bills, they were the genuine article.

Taggart had already reached the same conclusion. "We have to talk to Mr. McCoy. I'll need direction to this shack he's living in."

"You can't reach it by car."

"We'll take a helo."

From his seat on the arm of the sofa, Sam snorted. "Good luck trying to land on the mountainside. There's not a clear horizontal surface anywhere within twenty miles of the line shack. The only way to reach it is by horse."

"Or by all-terrain vehicle," Jake added slowly.

"Since when?" Sam wanted to know.

"I had the men cut a path up to the shack last year."

Taggart brought his head around, speculation rife in his dark eyes. "Go up there often, do you, Mr. Henderson?"

The question was so loaded that everyone in the room stiffened, including Rachel.

Jake replied with careful precision. "The last time Grizzly was in town, he admitted the winters were getting to him more than they used to. Shad and I made him see a doctor, who confirmed the old man had an irregular heartbeat. I had the path cut because I was worried that he might take sick and we wouldn't be able to get him down the mountain."

The two men waged a silent battle of wills. Taggart was the first to blink. "Do I need to arrange for an ATV?"

"We have four we use here at the ranch. Be here at eight tomorrow morning and I'll take you up."

"Tomorrow? What's wrong with right now?"

"It'll be dark in a few hours. You ever try to maneuver a four-wheeler up a mountainside at night?"

"All right, I get your point." Frustration at the delay razored through Taggart's voice. "I'll be here at eight."

"Shad will go with us."

Rachel jumped in before any of the other Hendersons could co-opt the fourth vehicle. "So will I."

"The hell you will," Jake retorted, leveling a

look in her direction at last. It wasn't a pleasant experience.

With a cool lift of her brow, Rachel returned his stare. "I beg your pardon?"

"It's eight hours up there and back."

"So?"

"If you think you ache after the little time you spent on a horse this afternoon, imagine what you'll feel like after eight hours on an ATV."

"I'll take along an extra supply of liniment."

A sudden flush stained his cheeks. For a wild moment, Rachel thought the provocative remark might penetrate the wall that had sprung up between them. Her hope crashed when Jake shrugged and turned away.

"Suit yourself."

Russ Taggart tried a more placating approach. "I really don't need you for this phase of the investigation, Rachel. I can take it from here."

"I've got as much a stake in the investigation at this point as you do. I'm going."

Rachel drove away from the Bar-H fifteen minutes later. Long, sharp shadows slanted across the gravel road. The air carried the same chill it had during her drive out to the ranch what now seemed like a lifetime ago.

The Hendersons, she reflected with a last look in

the rearview mirror, had acknowledged her arrival this morning with a good deal more friendliness than her departure this evening. None of them had offered to show her out. Jake hadn't even glanced her way.

Well, she couldn't blame anyone but herself for the frost in their manner. She'd gone along with Russ's scheme against her better judgment and wormed her way into their midst under false pretenses.

Okay, not totally false. She'd had her own reasons for wanting to get closer to Jake, and most of them revolved around the hunger that had tugged at her with long, relentless fingers.

The hunger was still there, low in her belly, wounded but not dead by any means. Like a slumbering beast that could stir to full, fierce wakefulness at a single prod. For that reason, and that reason only, Rachel was going to make the drive back out to the Bar-H tomorrow morning, drive up into the mountains, and plant her butt on the seat of an ATV.

She only hoped the seat was padded.

Her aunt echoed the same sentiments when Rachel announced the projected expedition. Setting aside the gory thriller she'd almost finished, Alice studied the niece sprawled on the couch.

"You're in for a hard ride, girl. You sure you know what you're doing?"

"No."

Her salt-and-pepper curls bouncing, the older woman shook her head. "I still don't understand what this is all about. Why do you have to talk to Shad's cousin?"

"We're hoping he may have some information related to the crash last year."

That was all Rachel could tell her. From necessity, Taggart had related a few sparse details to the Hendersons. In the process, he'd repeatedly stressed the need for containment. The last thing he wanted was for word of the missing millions to leak and a horde of modern-day prospectors to invade the area.

"Well, I think you traipsing up into the mountains like that is a damn fool idea," Alice said bluntly. "If you weren't going with Jake Henderson, I'd worry myself sick about you. And speaking of Jake…"

She cocked her head, her eyes shrewd. "You two seem to be getting along pretty good."

They'd been getting along much better before Taggart showed up this afternoon, her niece thought ruefully.

"He's a good man. Better, I'm guessing, than the one you came out here to get away from for a while."

A prick of conscience pushed Rachel to her feet. She needed to call Dale and she needed to do it tonight. Despite the mess she'd made of things this afternoon, one salient fact had emerged with crystal clarity. Jake Henderson made her feel more alive, more of a woman than she'd ever imagined it was possible to feel.

She'd never be able to settle for anything less now.

"I came out here to take care of you," she reminded her aunt with a wry grin. "And I'm not doing a very good job of it. Are you sure you'll be okay if I go with Jake tomorrow? I'll leave my cell phone with you and make sure Mrs. Hardwick from next door comes over to check up on you."

"I'm sure, I'm sure. You just watch yourself, girl. Anything can happen up there in the mountains."

Chapter 8

Rachel lay staring at the ceiling for a long time after her call to Dale Masters. To her chagrin, he'd accepted her decision to break things off between them with surprising aplomb. Evidently he'd used her absence to do some serious thinking, too. As he informed her in his own inimitable way, he'd concluded that her doubts and skittishness did not a healthy relationship make.

Okay, she could handle that. After all, she'd reached exactly the same conclusion. With only a twinge of regret she put the immediate past behind her, dragged the covers up to her chin, and concentrated on the immediate future.

She still hadn't fully recovered from the double whammy of Jake's fury at her deception coming so hard on the heels of those dizzying, sensual moments in Three Rock Canyon. She had no idea how—or *if*—she could regain the ground she'd lost with him after the fiasco with Russ Taggart, but she intended to give it her best shot. Even if it meant jouncing along on a four-wheeled minitractor for most of the day tomorrow.

She owed Henderson an apology, she decided after much tossing and turning, but once it was delivered she didn't intend to play the penitent. She'd ignored her instincts and gone along with Russ's need for subterfuge and secrecy. Yet as distasteful as her actions were to both Jake and Rachel herself, they were appropriate given the circumstances.

More or less.

Sighing, she shimmied down and dragged the covers over her head. She'd sort it out with Jake tomorrow.

Tomorrow came long before Rachel either expected or wanted it to. When the alarm clock dragged her from sleep at six-thirty, she grunted, lifted her head to check the time, and hit the snooze alarm. After a second and third buzz, she crawled out of bed.

She hadn't exaggerated when she'd told Jake

mornings weren't her favorite time of day. If she'd had any pull at all with Dale's boss, she would have urged the senator to sponsor a bill starting the work-day at noon. Trying to keep as quiet as possible, Rachel made her way down the creaky stairs and tiptoed past her aunt's bedroom to start the coffee. With one cup downed and one cup in hand, she felt human enough to tackle the challenge of getting dressed.

This time, she'd dress appropriately for the early morning chill. An oatmeal-colored turtleneck sweater in thin, fine wool provided a layer of warmth under her buttery soft suede jacket. Thick socks padded her hiking boots. Although she would have preferred wool slacks to jeans, she suspected the tough denim would do a better job at protecting her legs from underbrush.

She brought Alice a cup of coffee and, at her aunt's suggestion, detoured to the garage before she left for a pair of work gloves. Shivering in the dim light of the new day, she backed her convertible down the drive.

When the sports car bumped over the cattle guard and pulled into the Bar-H yard a half hour later, Taggart was waiting for her, as was Shad.

And Jake.

With the collar of the blue flannel shirt he wore under his sheepskin vest turned up and his black

The Silhouette Reader Service™ — Here's how it works:

Accepting your 2 free books and gift places you under no obligation to buy anything. You may keep the books and gift and return the shipping statement marked "cancel." If you do not cancel, about a month later we'll send you 6 additional novels and bill you just $3.80 each in the U.S., or $4.21 each in Canada, plus 25¢ shipping & handling per book and applicable taxes if any.* That's the complete price and — compared to cover prices of $4.50 each in the U.S. and $5.25 each in Canada — it's quite a bargain! You may cancel at any time, but if you choose to continue, every month we'll send you 6 more books, which you may either purchase at the discount price or return to us and cancel your subscription.

*Terms and prices subject to change without notice. Sales tax applicable in N.Y. Canadian residents will be charged applicable provincial taxes and GST.

If offer card is missing write to: Silhouette Reader Service, 3010 Walden Ave., P.O. Box 1867, Buffalo NY 14240-1867

NO POSTAGE
NECESSARY
IF MAILED
IN THE
UNITED STATES

BUSINESS REPLY MAIL
FIRST-CLASS MAIL   PERMIT NO. 717   BUFFALO, NY

POSTAGE WILL BE PAID BY ADDRESSEE

SILHOUETTE READER SERVICE
3010 WALDEN AVE
PO BOX 1867
BUFFALO NY 14240-9952

Play The Lucky Hearts Game

and get... FREE BOOKS & a FREE GIFT... YOURS to KEEP!

Yes! I have scratched off the silver card. Please send me my **2 FREE BOOKS** and **FREE MYSTERY GIFT**. I understand that I am under no obligation to purchase any books as explained on the back of this card.

Scratch Here!
then look below to see what your cards get you...

345 SDL DC4F   **245 SDL DC4A**

NAME   (PLEASE PRINT CLEARLY)

ADDRESS

APT.#   CITY

STATE/PROV.   ZIP/POSTAL CODE

Twenty-one gets you
2 FREE BOOKS and a
FREE MYSTERY GIFT!

Twenty gets you
2 FREE BOOKS!

Nineteen gets you
1 FREE BOOK!

TRY AGAIN!

Offer limited to one per household and not valid to current Silhouette Intimate Moments® subscribers. All orders subject to approval.

Visit us online at

www.eHarlequin.com

felt cowboy hat pulled down low, he looked big and tough and distinctly unfriendly.

"You're late."

"Not by my watch."

Her breezy reply snapped his brows together. He stared at her for several unfathomable seconds, then spun on one boot heel and strode off.

Rachel swallowed a sigh. In the growing light of the new morning, with the mountains throwing jagged shadows across the valley and her breath pearling on the frosty air, she had to admit the idea of apologizing had seemed easier last night than it did right now.

"We're takin' two trucks," Shad informed her in a voice noticeably lacking its former warmth. He jerked his chin toward the pickups. Each sported two ATVs lashed side by side in the truck beds. "You can ride with me."

"She's riding with me."

Jake reappeared and tossed what looked like a folded blanket into the truck bed.

"Ms. Quinn and I have a few matters to discuss."

Apparently Rachel would get her chance to apologize sooner than later. With a nod to Taggart, she climbed into the mud-streaked pickup.

Jake idled the engine and let Shad drive out first. Dust plumed behind the first truck, causing the second to lag well behind. So far behind, in fact, that a couple bends of the road soon cut off all sight of the lead vehicle. Rachel didn't attach any particular significance to its absence until Jake hit the brakes and brought the pickup to a halt smack in the middle of nowhere.

Or so it appeared to Rachel. A wire fence separated the gravel and dirt road from an unbroken vista of brown grass and stubby pine. In the distance, the purple mountains showed a dusting of white on their peaks.

Shoving the gearshift into park, Jake twisted the key and killed the engine. He angled to face her, then silence dropped like a stone. Rachel stood it as long as she could. Keeping her voice level, she launched into what she considered a calm and logical explanation.

"I worked on the accident task force for a good part of last year. The sequence of the bills carried aboard that plane was burned into my brain. The moment I saw the fifty you passed at the fair, I had to report it."

Under the brim of his hat, his rain-blue eyes skewed her to the truck seat. Rachel fought the urge to fiddle with the window button or look out across the mesa.

"I couldn't tell you that night at the fair. I *still* can't tell you the exact details. But I will tell you that my gut kept insisting you came by the fifty innocently.''

Her gut, and the hours she'd spent with this man. From what she'd learned in the past few days, Jake held true to himself, to his family and to the memory of his wife. Particularly to the memory of his wife. Resolutely, Rachel ignored the sharp little ping that thought caused just under her heart.

''Unfortunately, gut instinct doesn't carry as much weight in my line of work as much as field samples, laboratory tests and data analyses.''

The implication that he fell into the category of a field sample or lab test didn't sit particularly well with Jake. He didn't say a word, but his expression went from hard to downright dangerous.

Doggedly, Rachel plowed ahead. As much as she would have liked to, she couldn't put this whole mess off on Taggart. She'd gone along with him, even conducted a few discreet inquiries on her own.

''We gathered information on you,'' she told Jake. ''The information we collected raised a few questions.''

Questions that still hadn't been completely answered. Taggart had yet to verify the source of the infusion of cash into the Bar-H's operating account. Last night, a tight-jawed Jake had indicated that his brothers had provided the cash. As part owners, they shared the costs as well as the profits from the ranch. When Taggart informed them he'd already had someone checking their accounts, Marsh, Reece and Sam had agreed to provide proof of the money transfers...after they'd contacted their brother Evan and got the attorney's take on the situation. It had *not* been a friendly exchange.

"I accepted your invitation to dinner and came out to Bar-H with the deliberate intention of learning what I could about you," Rachel admitted. "And then..."

Then Jake had kissed her and short-circuited every system in her body.

"Then things got personal between us, and I decided to go with my gut after all."

For an analyst trained to consider every scrap of information with intense scrutiny, the admission that she'd fallen back to instinct rather than data came hard for Rachel. Very hard. But there was no other way to explain her reaction every time Jake Henderson took her in his arms.

"Are you finished?"

"Yes. No."

Chewing on her lower lip, she dragged out the apology she'd rehearsed last night. It didn't sound any better now than it had then.

"I'm sorry, Jake. I shouldn't have allowed myself to mix personal interests with professional responsibilities. It wasn't fair to you, and it confused the hell out of me. All right,'' she said, bracing herself for the blast she was sure would follow. "I'm done. Your turn."

Jake didn't disappoint her. With an anger made even more potent because he kept it so tightly controlled, he cut right to the quick.

"I told you Ellen was the only woman in my life, so she's all I really have to measure things by. She never lied to me, not once in all our years together. Not that I know of, anyway."

Well, bully for Ellen!

The irreverent retort popped into Rachel's head. Thankfully, she had just enough sense to keep it from popping *out* of her mouth.

"I couldn't have loved her the way I did if she had," Jake finished tightly.

That hurt. More than Rachel wanted to admit. She fumbled for something to say and found herself resorting to Russ Taggart's specious argument.

"I didn't lie to you, Jake. I just sort of filtered the truth."

The scornful twist of his mouth told her what he thought of that sorry excuse.

"We're going up to find Grizzly," he said, enunciating each syllable with exaggerated care. "We'll try to get him to remember where he picked up those bills. We'll close out my part in this fiasco, and you'll apologize to my family for dragging them into this.''

"Fair enough.''

"And then, Ms. Quinn, we'll talk about where we go from there.''

Her stomach jumped. Cocking her head, she met his gaze head-on.

"Just out of curiosity, where do you think we *can* go from there?''

"I'm damned if I know. Without trust, we don't have much of foundation to build on.''

Ouch! Henderson could deliver a helluva punch when he wanted to. Well, Rachel refused to grovel any longer. What was done was done, and she couldn't undo it.

"I'll tell you what,'' she said with a lift of one shoulder. ''You let me know when you decide whether you can trust me again, and I'll let you know whether I care.''

As it had earlier this morning, her breezy reply took Jake aback. Good grief, hadn't the always perfect Saint Ellen ever stood up to him?

Not very often, apparently. Ignoring the tight grooves bracketing his mouth, Rachel flapped a hand.

"You'd better move it, cowboy. As you pointed out last night, it's a long ride up to this cabin.''

* * *

They found Shad and Taggart waiting for them at a pull-off cut into the side of a slope. A barely discernable dirt track wound upward, cutting through a maze of mountain laurel and tall pines.

Shad had already unloaded his two ATVs and strolled forward to help Jake. Attaching a light-weight, tri-fold ramp to the pickup's tailgate, they maneuvered the four-wheelers out of the truck. Mud-splashed and well-dented, the ATVs were equipped with an assortment of accessories that included rear carriers, brush guards, winches, utility lights, extra fuel containers and front mounts for snowplows.

But it was the high-impact plastic scabbard Jake retrieved from the back of the pickup that snagged Taggart's attention. Eyes hooded, he watched while the rancher opened the case and checked the rifle nestled inside. His gaze lingered on the high-powered scope clamped onto the stock.

"That's a Clarion scope, isn't it?"

"Yes." Jake flicked him a cool glance. "An X-93."

"Pretty powerful piece of equipment. The last time I saw one of those, we took it off a dead sniper."

"That right?"

The deliberately disinterested drawl brought spots of color into Russ's cheeks. He started forward, came up short when Jake flashed him a warning look. For a moment, something so close to animosity arced between the two men that Rachel sucked in a gulp of the chill, pine-scented air.

Unlocking his jaw, Taggart managed a credible drawl of his own. ''Too bad the X-93 doesn't accommodate an infrared targeting system.''

Sliding his hand inside his down-filled red vest, he withdrew an automatic. Rachel knew next to nothing about guns, but she'd once heard Russ describe his as blue steel death. With seeming casualness, he aimed at a nearby tree branch and thumbed a lever. A bright red beam lasered through the air and tattooed a small, round circle on the chest of a squirrel watching the proceedings with wide-eyed interest.

Taggart held the bead for a second or two before thumbing the switch again. The bright red circle disappeared. Sliding the automatic back inside his vest, the agent brought his cool gaze back around to Jake.

Rachel bit her lip. She couldn't help thinking this little demonstration was something Jake's two-year-old nephew might have indulged in. You show me your intergalactic ray gun or pee-pee or whatever, and I'll show you mine. It might have been funny if the message conveyed wasn't so unsettling.

Henderson was still on Taggart's list of suspects.

He'd *stay* on the list until he presented the FBI agent with incontrovertible proof he didn't belong there. And neither of them was prepared to trust the other until that happened.

Trust.

There it was again. With a grimace, Rachel folded her arms and waited while Jake snapped the rifle case shut and attached it barrel-down to the side of the ATV. Unsmiling, he strode over to check her out on the vehicle.

"It's pretty basic. The controls are in the handle-bars. You throttle up to increase speed, throttle back to slow."

"Got it."

"Watch the angle of the inclines. Of necessity, ATVs have high-set chassis to get over rough ter-rain. Even with their wide axles, they can tip and roll. Stay behind me and follow where I lead."

"Yes, sir!"

He hadn't thawed toward her yet. Not enough to find her flippant reply the least amusing, anyway. He strode back to his own vehicle and swung into the saddle. A twist of the throttles produced a muted roar, and Jake started up the sloping path. Cau-tiously, Rachel applied power and did the same. Taggart followed, with Shad bringing up the rear.

For the first half hour or so, she concentrated on maneuvering under low-hanging branches, around rock outcroppings, and over tree roots. For the second half hour, she actually enjoyed herself.

The scenery was spectacular. Tall, soaring pines in a dozen different shades of green speared into a sky so blue it might have been painted in acrylic. Beneath the pines, the dense underbrush offered patches of glossy red berries and an occasional clump of dark purple wildflowers. Every so often, the dirt path backtracked and the trees thinned enough to show glimpses of the slope they'd just climbed. The drop seemed a lot more vertical looking down than it had looking up.

Only after she'd been jouncing along for nearly an hour did Rachel decide that the ATV's cushioned seat could have used another inch or so of padding. When Jake throttled back and rolled to a stop in a small, grassy clearing, she was ready for a break. So was her bladder. She shouldn't have downed that extra cup of coffee before driving out to the Bar-H.

When Rachel threw her leg over the seat and dismounted, muscles still stiff from her hours on a horse yesterday afternoon registered an instant protest. She glanced around, spotted a thick-trunked tree at the edge of the clearing that would suit her purposes, and wished to heck she'd thought to stuff some tissue or a wad of toilet paper in her jacket pocket.

Jake must have read her mind. Either that, or he caught the longing glance she gave the tree.

"Check the carrier on the back of your ATV. We pack a stash of emergency supplies whenever we head up into the mountains. I think Sydney stuck in a few extra items the last time she rode out with us."

The emergency supplies, Rachel saw as she rooted around in the hard-cased carrier, included walkie-talkies, a first aid kit, a fold-up tool pack, a Swiss Army knife, a flashlight and matches, a tube of expensive sunblock and—bless Sydney!—a half-dozen packages of moistened towelettes.

Clutching her prize, Rachel made a dash for the tree. She rejoined the men a short time later, refreshed and ready to resume the bumpy ride.

The novelty of crawling up the side of a mountain on a four-wheeler wore off at about the same time the dirt path deteriorated into little more than a trail of sawed-off tree stumps. From there on out, maneuvering her vehicle was sheer work. Rachel played constantly with the handlebar controls, piling on power for the climbs, throttling back to keep from pitching over when the slope angled.

She was sweating when they took the next breather. Shimmying out of her suede jacket, she stuffed it into the carrier and gulped down some of

Twice in a Lifetime

the bottled water Shad had packed. By the time the ramshackle cabin tucked amid a stand of ponderosa pine came into view, she couldn't ever remember being so thankful to see signs of civilization in her life.

As Jake had warned, the place was little more than a cracker box of weathered boards capped by a tin roof. Saplings with their branches hacked off supported a sagging porch. Two of the panes in the front window had cracked and were webbed with masking tape.

One by one, the ATVs slowed to a stop in the small clearing in front of the cabin. The engines idled and coughed before dying. Exhaust sullied the purity of the high mountain air. Stifling a groan, Rachel swung her leg over the seat. She was testing her legs when Jake issued a low, terse warning.

"Stay on the four-wheeler."

"What?"

"Get back."

"I don't... Good God!"

Her heart jumped into her throat. She stumbled back, her gaze locked on the black snout that poked through the crack of the opened front door.

"Damn," Taggart muttered, sliding his hand inside his vest toward his automatic.

"Stay easy!" Jake ordered sharply.

The long, pointed muzzle poked out another

inch. It was followed in short order by a small head, shaggy forepaws, and massive, humped shoulders.

"Is that the grizzly your cousin adopted?" Rachel murmured to Shad, sincerely hoping that proved to be the case.

"Looks like him. But he's really an American black, not a grizzly. Some fool slapped Isaac with that nickname when he took in the cub and it just sorta stuck to them both."

Since she had no particular desire to get up close and personal with either an American black *or* a grizzly, Rachel merely nodded and kept back.

"Wonder what he's doing at the cabin?" Shad mused. "This late in the season, he's usually out rooting up food twenty, twenty-four hours a day to get ready for hibernation."

Keeping both his stance and his voice nonthreatening, the foreman called out to his cousin. "Isaac, it's me, Shad."

The only answer was a growl from the bear. The weathered boards on the porch creaked under its weight as it began to rock from side to side.

"Jake's with me, Isaac. Call off your watchdog."

The animal emitted another growl, only this one started low and slowly escalated into a keening howl that lifted the hairs on the back of Rachel's neck.

"What the hell?" Shad muttered. "Hey, Isaac! You in there, pardner?"

He was in there, they discovered when the bear finally ceased its eerie wail and shuffled out the door. With a last look over his shoulder at the cabin, it disappeared into the pines behind the cabin.

Rachel kept a wary eye on the trees as she followed the men to the cabin. The odor reached her before she'd stepped onto the porch. She didn't need Jake's restraining hand to pull up short. She'd participated in enough on-scene accident investigations during her early days with the NTSB to recognize the stench of putrefying flesh.

Chapter 9

"A man dies in his own bed," Shad mused to Rachel, "his best friend standing watch over him. Not a bad way to go, all things considered."

Rachel nodded mutely in reply. She'd been sitting beside Shad on the trunk of a fallen tree for over an hour now. Patiently, the foreman carved another swirl on the knotty root he'd been whittling on while they waited for the arrival of a Coconino County deputy sheriff.

It looked to be a long wait. Taggart had used the radio he'd brought with him to contact his Denver office, which in turn had notified the Coconino County sheriff's office. Although it appeared

Shad's cousin had died of natural causes, the medical examiner would have to make the official determination. Or in this instance, the deputy sheriff who acted as a trained investigator for the ME when time, distance, or circumstances demanded. Marsh was bringing the deputy up to the shack to view the body and make his report. Then Shad intended to bury his cousin amid the mountains he loved.

"It was something, the way that bear stood guard over ole Isaac. He would have been feedin' the coyotes sure as shootin' if that pet of his hadn't kept them all away."

Rachel shifted to find a more comfortable perch on the fallen log. "How long do you think the bear would have stayed with your cousin if we hadn't showed up?"

"Don't rightly know." A tiny wood chip curled under Shad's knife blade. "With winter comin' on, he could've gone into hibernation and dozed off right there in the shack."

Rachel threw a glance at the cabin. Even with the door and windows opened wide, the stench was still overpowering. How in the world could Taggart stay inside? He'd been in the line shack most of the past hour, his handkerchief tied over his nose and mouth, probing the walls, the floorboard, the nooks and crannies under the tin roof.

Rachel shook her head, marveling at the agent's

dedication. She'd recognized that he was driven when she'd worked with him last year, but to conduct a field search under these conditions went above and beyond the call of duty.

Her gaze slid from the shadowy interior of the cabin to the man leaning against the porch rail. Jake had opted to remain outside, where the air was at least breathable. Arms folded, eyes intent under the brim of his black hat, he observed Taggart's progress.

"Jake Henderson didn't have nothin' to do with that airplane crash."

The absolute conviction in Shad McCoy's voice swung Rachel's head around. "I know."

"I watched him grow from a skinny, knock-kneed grasshopper to the man he is now." Another wood shaving joined the pile between Shad's boots. "He'd cut off his arm before he'd do intentional harm to man or beast."

"I know."

The knife paused. The foreman peered at her thoughtfully. "You tell him that, missy?"

"I tried. He wasn't in the mood to listen."

Shad chewed on that for a while. "Give him time," he advised after a moment or two. "Jake can be stubborn as a brick wall when he sets his mind to it."

"So I've discovered."

Stubborn and loyal and too damned disturbing for Rachel's peace of mind. She'd almost lost it in his arms at the bottom of a canyon, for Pete's sake. If she'd had her way, they would have gotten down and dirty right there, rocks and all. Her nipples tingling at the memory, she glanced up to find Shad watching her with a bemused expression.

"What?"

"I'm thinkin' you might be good for Jake, after all. He needs shakin' up, and you sure been doin' some serious shakin', missy."

That was one way to put it, Rachel supposed. But where the shaking would lead was still anyone's guess. She was mulling over the less-than-satisfactory situation when a muffled exclamation floated to them through the open cabin windows.

Taggart stumbled through the door. His dark eyes blazed above the handkerchief that covered his nose and mouth. He rushed across the clearing clutching what looked like a burlap-wrapped bundle.

"Look at this!"

Her nerves igniting, Rachel jumped up and threw Jake a swift glance. He followed more slowly, showing no emotion as Taggart jerked down his mask, dragged in a long breath, and fumbled back the burlap folds.

"It's a full brick," he exclaimed in fierce satisfaction. "Give or take a few bills."

Excitement pumped hot and swift into Rachel's veins. A brick, she'd learned during the investigation, was what came off the line after guillotine-style cutters sliced the newly printed sheets of banknotes. The high-speed blades diced a hundred sheets at a time, first into two units, then into four, finally into individual stacks. The one-hundred note stacks were then banded and packaged into bricks. Each brick contained forty stacks, which meant...

She performed a quick mental calculation and gulped. Russ Taggart was holding approximately two hundred thousand dollars in newly printed fifty-dollar bills in his hands.

"McCoy found it." The FBI operative's entire body vibrated with elation. "He found the damned container."

He shared an exultant, wolfish grin with Rachel before his glance collided with Jake's.

"What container?"

Like a paper bag crushed between two fists, Russ's glee folded in on itself. Still hefting the brick in one hand, he faced the taut, square-shouldered rancher.

"I'm not cleared to..."

"Don't even *think* about laying that kind of bureaucratic bull on me, Taggart."

Still the agent hesitated, unwilling even now to

share specific details of the crash with anyone outside the inner circle of investigators.

"You're standing on my land," Jake reminded
him grimly. "Holding money that belonged to Isaac
McCoy. It now belongs to Shad, as Grizzly's only
living next of kin, unless or until you prove otherwise."

"The hell it does! All it will take is one call from
me to certify the authenticity of these bills."

"And all it will take is one call from me to my
brother Evan to tie you and that stack of bills up in
so many legal knots it'll take you ten years to un-
tangle them."

Dislike flared in the agent's eyes, so dark and
intense that unease fluttered in Rachel's chest.

"I want to know the whole story, Taggart.
Now."

It was a stand-off. Two gunfighters facing each
other on a deserted street at high noon. The problem
was, they were both supposed to be the good guys.

"Tell him," Rachel said tersely. "If you don't,
I will."

"All right, all right." Clearly put out at having
his hand forced, Taggart conceded. "I told you that
the fifty you passed came from the downed aircraft.
What I couldn't tell you was that it was part of a
shipment of newly printed bills. They were on their
way to the Federal Reserve Bank in Salt Lake City

when the DC-10 went down. The bills were sealed in a special container, which we didn't find at or anywhere near the crash site. We think the container was dropped some minutes before the plane plowed into the mountain."

"Dropped?" Jake's brows slashed together. "In midflight?"

Rachel could see him struggling to make sense of it.

"The crew had to be pretty desperate to dump their cargo in midair. What were they, off-course and low on fuel or something?"

"Or something," Taggart bit out.

Rachel stepped in before the animosity simmering between the two men could erupt again.

"We recovered the DC-10's flight recorder," she told Jake. "That, plus the evidence that was gathered on-scene indicate someone blew the cargo hatch and caused the plane to suddenly decompress."

Her analysis of the damage to the composite materials of the plane's undercarriage had helped confirm that theory, but she saw no need to mention that now.

"The pilots were forced to use emergency measures to bring their aircraft down to a safe altitude. The snowstorm obscured their visibility, and in a critical moment of distraction, they flew into the mountainside.''

It didn't take Jake long to piece the puzzle together. ''Are you telling me someone deliberately blew a cargo hatch in midair? To eject this container of money?''

''That's our best guess. We speculate that whoever disabled the security mechanisms and ejected the pod may have put a tracking device on it, intending to drop it to an accomplice on the ground. Either that, or he planned to follow the container out the cargo hatch and parachute down with it. If so, he didn't make it out of the aircraft in time. All four crew members died in the crash.''

''Can't imagine anyone fool enough to consider jumping out of a plane over the Rockies,'' Shad commented. ''How much was in this here pod, anyway?''

With a glance at the tight-lipped Russ, Rachel supplied the answer. ''Forty million dollars.''

''Ho-ly Hell!''

''Teams scoured the mountains within a hundred-mile radius of the crash site,'' she told the astonished foreman. ''The pod was never located. Nor did any of the bills it contained show up in circulation until...''

''Until I paid for a beer and a soda at the county fair,'' Jake finished grimly.

Shad tipped his hat forward and scratched his head, still stunned by the idea of forty million dollars dropping out of the sky. "Ole Isaac must have stumbled on the money during his wanderings."

"Wanderings?" Taggart jumped back into the conversation. "Where did he wander?"

"All over these mountains. Him and that bear of his. A full-growed American black will stake out a territory of thirty, maybe forty square miles, but he'll prowl a whole lot farther in search of female companionship come mating season. Most times, Isaac prowled with him."

Taggart swore, low and viciously.

Rachel guessed what was running through his head. More teams. More search grids drawn across a map. More weeks or possibly months of climbing down steep gullies and up sheer cliff faces.

"The container was banded and sealed," she said, thinking aloud. "It must have broken open on impact. My guess is that Shad's cousin transported the money brick by brick to a safe place."

"It's not in the cabin," Taggart stated. "I pretty well tore the place apart, but only found this one brick." He eyed the stack in his hands before giving Shad a look that was half question, half plea. "Any idea where your cousin might have stashed the rest?"

"Hell, he could have stuck it anywhere. There

are hundreds of hidey-holes and caves around these parts. Mountain cats inhabit half of them. The rest are home to bears and skunks and other inhospitable varmints you don't want to walk in on unannounced.''

Like a man grabbing at a lifeline, Taggart latched onto the idea of a cave. "What about the bear your cousin adopted? The old man would have known the location of his den. Think he might have hidden the money there?"

"It's a possibility." Shad skimmed the rugged peaks around them with a look that mingled respect and regret. "Where that den is, though, is anybody's guess."

Rachel could almost hear Russ's mind clicking off the calls he'd have to make. One to the U.S. Fish and Wildlife Service. Another to the FBI's resident expert on bears, whoever that might be. Still more calls to hunters and trackers in the local area to assist in the search. So she wasn't surprised when Russ laid a thoughtful look on Jake.

"You pack a first-class hunting rifle, Henderson. You ever hunt these mountains?"

"Occasionally."

"I don't suppose I can convince you to track McCoy's bear for me."

"You can try."

* * *

When Marsh Henderson and Coconino Country Deputy Sheriff Buck Silverthorne arrived on the scene, afternoon was rolling into evening. They roared into the clearing on ATV's piled high with bedrolls and equipment…including, Rachel saw as they unloaded, a rubberized body bag.

The sun had already dipped behind the peaks. The temperature had dropped a good twenty degrees. It seemed to drop another ten when Jake introduced Silverthorne to Russ Taggart. The deputy wasn't particularly happy about the fact that the Feds had launched an operation in Coconino County without prior coordination.

"I was merely following up on a lead in an ongoing investigation," Taggart said with a shrug that wouldn't help cement relations. "Until a few hours ago, there was nothing to coordinate."

"Well, my boss says I'm to hang around and 'assist' the effort," Silverthorne told him.

"Fine. We can use all the help we can get."

"First things first, though. Where's ole Grizzly's body?"

Reclaiming their seats on the fallen log, Rachel and Shad watched from a distance while the others donned protective masks and made brief forays into the cabin.

Each time the deputy came out for air, his radio

crackled with static as he reported his findings to the medical examiner. Dusk was painting the cabin in dark shadows when the ME concurred in Silverthorne's recommendation of death from natural causes and released the body for burial.

Hunching his shoulders, Shad scowled at the zippered bag the men carried out of the cabin. "Don't seem right, though, buryin' Isaac in that thing."

"Marsh and I will tear some boards from the cabin walls in the morning and nail together a coffin," Jake promised.

"Guess I'll have to go through his belongings in the morning, too." With a creak of arthritic joints, the foreman pushed to his feet. "Place should be aired out by then."

"I'll help you," Rachel offered.

Poking through a dead man's belongings didn't rank particularly high on her list of favorite activities, but she wasn't used to sitting around on the sidelines twiddling her thumbs.

Shad accepted her offer with gruff thanks. Jake, however, read more into it than mere politeness.

"Going to look for evidence Taggart might have missed?"

Heat warmed her cheeks. Shoving off the log, she looked him square in the eye. "Okay, I deserve that hit. It's the last one I'm going to take about this business, though, from you or anyone else. And just to set the record straight, Henderson, I was merely trying to make myself useful.''

Satisfied she'd made her point, Rachel dusted the seat of her jeans and announced she was going to wash up.

Jake set his jaw, his narrowed gaze on her back as she trudged across the clearing to the stream trickling down a slick rock surface. He could have suggested a dozen ways for the woman to make herself useful, not the least of which were laying out the bedrolls and opening some of the cans he and Marsh had retrieved from the cabin. Ellen would have already had the beans simmering, the Spam sizzling and the coffee boiling.

But Rachel wasn't Ellen. That had been brought home to Jake in a dozen different ways since the night of the fair. She was tough where Ellen was soft, too stubborn to admit she couldn't ride a horse or sit on an ATV for hours, and damnably arousing instead of enticing. Even more to the point, Jake knew her well enough by now to suspect she wouldn't take kindly to the suggestion that the only female in the group take care of the housekeeping chores. Hell, she'd probably report him for sexual harassment.

Grimacing, Jake rubbed the back of his neck. Okay, maybe that last bit was unfair. But the fact that she'd reported him to the FBI still rankled.

That, and the realization of how close he'd come to making a fool of himself over the woman.

How close he still was.

Annoyed by the way his gaze lingered on her trim, rounded rear as she bent over to swish her hands in the trickling water, he turned to his brother.

"After Shad finishes going through Grizzly's things tomorrow, I want you to take him and Rachel back down. I think I'll stick around here for a while."

Hooking his thumbs in his belt, Marsh eyed him speculatively. "Are you going to track the bear and find Taggart's missing millions for him?"

"Could be. And could be I just want to make sure none of those bricks mysteriously disappear, leaving me the prime suspect in this little drama once again."

His brother's gaze sharpened. He flicked a glance at the FBI agent hunched over his radio and lowered his voice. "You think Taggart would set you up like that?"

"No. But I don't trust him, despite everything he and Rachel told me this morning."

Assuming they'd leveled with him, of course. The idea that Rachel might still be holding back vital information got halfway down Jake's craw and stuck there. When he admitted as much to his brother, Marsh revealed that he'd called a few friends in D.C. this morning to check on Rachel Quinn.

"From all reports, she's got a reputation for straight shooting at the National Transportation and Safety Board. I've been trying to square that reputation in my mind with the way she lied to us."

"According to Ms. Quinn," Jake drawled, "she didn't lie. She merely filtered the truth."

Marsh scraped a hand across his jaw. "Guess we all do that on occasion. I sure filtered like hell the first time I met Lauren."

The comparison hit home. As his wife told the story, Marsh had rushed to her rescue during an attempted break-in at her sister's house. Unfortunately, he neglected to mention until much later that he was the one who'd staged the break-in in the first place.

Since Marsh had been tracking the hit men who'd missed their intended target and gunned Ellen down instead, Jake found no fault at all with his brother's tactics. But Evan, the lawyer in the family, had let his brother know in graphic and distinctly unlawyerly terms what he thought of that bit of illegal evidence gathering.

"If you look at it that way, Rachel was only going for the greater good," Marsh said. "Just as

158 _Twice in a Lifetime_

I was when I set up Lauren. Maybe we should cut her some slack.''

A noncommittal grunt was the only response.

''The lady's no lightweight, Jake.''

Coming from Marsh, that was high praise. And at least partially deserved in this case. Jake couldn't name any other woman who could have met his anger head-on this morning and tossed it right back at him when her own temper sparked. Or made the long, jarring ride up the mountain without a single complaint. Or handled the sight of Grizzly's putrefying corpse without losing her breakfast.

No, he admitted silently, Rachel wasn't Ellen. Rachel Quinn was her own woman.

That thought was still kicking around in Jake's head when she slid into the bedroll beside his some hours later.

By mutual consent, everyone in the party had opted not to eat or sleep in the cabin. There wasn't enough room, for one thing. For another, the air inside still carried the reek of death. A meal cooked over a campfire and the bedrolls Marsh had strapped onto his ATV held far more appeal.

The sleeping bags had been spread out under the bright, cold palette of stars. Rachel snuggled into the sleeping bag Jake had placed between his own and Marsh's. He figured she'd have trouble sleeping on the hard ground, but not three minutes later, she flopped over onto her stomach, mumbled something into the suede jacket she'd bundled to use for a pillow and blew out a long, tremulous breath. Another fluttery sigh followed, then another. It took Jake a moment or two to realize she'd gone out like a light.

Folding one arm under his head, he tried to blank his mind to the sound of her breathing. As soft as those whispery sighs were, they crowded out the crackling fire, the wind rustling through the pines, even Shad's rhythmic grunts and Buck Silverthorne's whistling snores.

The image of the woman issuing those little puffs crowded out everything else. All it took was a slight shift of his head where it rested on the crook of his elbow, and she filled Jake's view. Her face was a pale oval, her lashes dark shadows against her cheeks. The hair that spilled over her suede jacket had Jake clenching his fists to keep from snaking out a hand and snagging a tangled strand.

Dammit, he didn't want to want her. Wasn't sure if he could ever trust her again. So why was he lying here with his insides tied up in knots? And why the devil did he have to battle the urge to reach over, drag down that zipper and tumble the woman into his arms?

Disgusted with the ache that pierced him at the

idea of Rachel's body slick and hot under his, Jake
turned his head away from the sleeping woman and
stared up at the indigo sky. After another five or
ten minutes with the sound of her breathless little
sighs thundering in his ear, he started counting the
stars.

Chapter 10

Jake woke with a crick in his neck, the dawn cold and frosty on his cheeks, and Rachel snuggled into his side. Sometime during the night, she'd flopped over again and rolled right up against him.

Or he had followed through on the urge that had kept him hard and hurting for what felt like hours last night and dragged her into his arms.

However she'd arrived there, Jake felt no inclination to disturb her. Her head stayed tucked between his shoulder and chin. Her long, slender curves followed his contours as if they'd been sculpted to match his.

He waited for the rush of guilt, the inevitable

comparison between the way Rachel fit so perfectly against him and the way he'd had to contort his six-feet-plus to accommodate Ellen's slighter build.

The guilt didn't come. Nor did much more than a fleeting thought of his wife linger in his mind.

Instead, an unaccustomed sense of ease seeped through him, as though someone had lightened a burden he'd carried for longer than he could remember. Despite the remnants of the anger he still nursed against Rachel, it felt right to hold her in the quiet of the dawn, with the cold mists rising from the warm earth beneath them, and listen to the rhythm of her soft, snuffling breath. Or it did until she gave a jerky spasm, raised her head, and blinked at him owlishly.

"Whatimeizit?"

"Early. Go back to sleep."

"Uhnnh."

Fighting an arm free of the zippered bag, she threw it across his chest and dropped back down. She was asleep before her head hit his shoulder.

Jake stiffened. Holding a sleepy, pliant Rachel curved against his side was one thing. Holding her half sprawled across his chest was something else. One by one his muscles coiled. Sweat started to pool at the base of his spine. He considered yanking down the zipper of his sleeping bag to let the chilly dawn hose him down, but Rachel's left breast was planted right over the damned pull.

By the time he heard Marsh start to stir, Jake was hard and hurting all over again. With a grunt that was half regret and half relief, he eased Rachel off his chest and onto her back. It took some doing to tuck her arm back inside her sleeping bag. She wasn't exactly a restful sleeper.

"Got her all zipped up again?"

He glanced over and found Marsh watching the proceedings with undisguised interest. The beginnings of a grin creased his brother's unshaven cheeks as he untangled himself from his own bedroll and joined Jake at the iced-over stream.

"I see you followed my advice and cut the lady some slack."

"Maybe." Jake rapped his knuckles on the thin ice to break it. "And maybe she just got cold."

"Yeah, right. You sure you want me to take her and Shad back down the mountain this morning? I'll be happy to hang around here and keep an eye on our friend Taggart while you warm Ms. Quinn up a little more."

"I'll stay. I'm the one who led Taggart here. I'll see this thing through."

Jake stuck to that intention through most of the morning.

As promised, he and Marsh pried boards off the cabin walls to construct a rough coffin. Buck Silverthorne helped, as did Russ Taggart. Jake might have appreciated the FBI agent's willingness to pitch in if he didn't suspect Taggart was merely continuing his search by tearing apart the cabin.

While the men worked, Rachel helped Shad sort through his cousin's personal possessions. They found pitifully few. A tattered bible. Three plaid shirts, worn jeans and long johns. A bulky winter parka of greased elk hide with the hair side sewn in. A shoebox containing a jumble of fishing tackle, matches, a broken jackknife and a military medal in the shape of a silver star.

The medal's frayed, blue-and-white ribbon fluttered in the breeze when Shad carried it to the grave Marsh and Jake had dug on a high slope. The site provided an unobstructed view of the surrounding mountains.

"Isaac got this in Korea," he told the small group that assembled for the burial. "For gallantry in action."

When Jake placed it atop the makeshift coffin, Shad dragged off his hat. The wind played with his sparse gray hair as he offered a simple eulogy.

"Here lies Isaac McCoy. He was a good man, if a mite confused in his last years. Take care of him, Lord."

After a short, respectful silence, Taggart and Buck Silverthorne drifted away. Rachel paused to lay a clump of feathery, late-blooming purple blazing star beside the military medal. Then she, too, left the men of the Bar-H to finish taking care of their own.

Jake clamped a hand on Shad's thin, stooped shoulder. He didn't like the thought that the foreman was older than his cousin and just as likely to go at any time.

"We'll come back up with a proper marker."

"Isaac doesn't need a stone. He's got his mountains. You boys finish up here. I'll go pack the rest of his gear."

Retrieving his spade, Jake went to work. Marsh soon joined him. They shoveled the mounded dirt in the sure, smooth rhythm of men well used to working together. With the sun beating down and the squirrels chattering from the branches, Jake couldn't help but remember another graveside service.

"You okay?"

He looked up, read the sympathy and concern in his brother's eyes.

"Yeah," he answered slowly. "I'm okay."

He was okay, Jake realized. The past didn't eat at his soul the way it usually did. The hurt would

always be there, just under his ribs, but memories
of Ellen now brought more pleasure than pain.

Much of that he owed to Rachel, Jake admitted
grudgingly. Although he wasn't quite sure what had
killed the anger she'd fired in him by her deception,
it had pretty much run its course.

Pretty much. Enough still lingered to make him
eye her warily when she approached him while he
was helping load the last of the gear on the ATVs.

"I need to talk to you."

"I'm listening."

"Not here."

With a glance at the others, she led the way into
the trees. Dried pine needles crunched underfoot.
Overhead, the breeze sighed through the high
branches. When they were far enough away to en-
sure privacy, she stopped and turned.

"Is there a copper mine anywhere around here?"

Of all the questions Jake might have expected
from her, that wasn't one of them.

"Over on the next ridge," he answered. "It was
abandoned years ago, after the copper played out.
Why?"

"Is the mine on Bar-H property?"

"Yes."

"Damn! I was afraid of that."

"What's the problem here? The mine's on our

land, but Big John sold the mineral rights to the
Arizona Mining Company before I was born.''

She chewed on her lower lip for several moments
before seeming to reach a decision. ''Give me your
hand.''

Wondering what the hell this was all about, Jake
complied. Her fingers closed over his wrist and
turned his hand palm up. She held up a tight-
clenched fist and opened her fingers, one by one. A
shower of small, mud-covered pebbles dropped into
his hand.

''Take a look.''

He raised his hand, trying to catch the spare sunlight that filtered through the pines. ''It might help
if you tell me what I'm looking for.''

With a cluck of impatience, she stepped closer.
Her breath warmed his skin as she tilted his hand
this way and that. ''There. See that sheen?''

It took him a moment to spot the dull green pa-
tina showing through the mud on several of the pebbles. Although he'd never been personally involved
in any of the mining operations scattered across Arizona, Jake recognized it immediately.

''Looks like copper ore.''

''It is. A high-grade sulfide ore, to be exact.''

Curiosity had him slanting her a quick look.
''You know about copper mining?''

''I know very little about mining, but I do know

materials. That's my specialty, remember? I recognized these samples the minute I found them.''

"Okay, I'll bite. Where did you find them?''

"They were stuck in the mud caked in the grooves of Grizzly's boots.''

His fingers closed over the nuggets. He had a guess where this was going, but asked anyway. "What are you thinking, Rachel?''

"I'm thinking that an abandoned mine might be a great place to hide a stash of money.''

Jake considered that in silence. She waited impatiently for his reaction. When it didn't come, she shoved her fingers through her hair and raked the dark fall back from her face.

"Okay, I'm reaching here, but an abandoned mine is as good a place to start looking as any other. Can you find your way to it?''

"I know the way,'' he answered slowly, searching her face. "What I don't know is why you've come to me with your discovery instead of Russ Taggart.''

She looked away. Her sable lashes fanned her cheeks. Jake was so close he saw the gold tipping their ends...and the sincerity in her hazel eyes when she raised them to his again.

"I owe you, Jake. I got you into this mess. I want to help get you out. If I tell Taggart about these nuggets, he'll send his whole team swarming through the mine. He might even put you at the head of his suspect list again, since it's on Bar-H property.''

Jake figured there wasn't much ''might'' about it.

''It's a long shot to think the money could be there,'' Rachel said intently. ''But if it is, we'll find it, report its location to Taggart and his team, and be done with the whole, blasted business.''

''Forty million dollars is a hell of a stash. What if I decide I want to keep a million or two?''

''You won't.''

''You sure about that?''

''I'm sure.''

The flat assertion went a long way to making up for the past few days, but Jake couldn't resist digging the needle in one more time.

''You've already turned me in to the FBI once. Why are you so willing to trust me now?''

''I told you why yesterday morning, but you were too ticked off at the time to listen. I'm going with my gut where you're concerned, Henderson.''

It was hardly a soft, passionate promise of love or devotion, but it started a heat just below Jake's belt. She was right. He'd allowed his anger over her seeming betrayal to get him all wrapped around the fence pole. He should have gone with his gut, as she did.

If he hadn't stepped on it too badly, maybe he still could. Dropping the ore nuggets into his pocket, Jake reached out and tunneled a hand through the hair lying thick and heavy on the back of her neck.

"If you're prepared to follow your instincts, Quinn, I guess I can do the same."

Surprise and a hint of wariness flashed in her eyes. Splaying a hand against his chest, she tossed his words back at him.

"Are *you* sure about this, Jake?"

"I'm sure."

"Why?" Still suspicious, she held him off. "What caused the change of heart?"

"I did a lot of thinking last night. And this morning, when I woke up to find you'd burrowed up against me."

"I burrowed?"

"You did."

"Hmm. I can't believe I slept right through it."

He suspected she could sleep through a hurricane but this wasn't the time to tell her so.

"What conclusion did you reach after all this thinking?" she asked.

He thought of all the answers he could give to that one and pared them down to the only one that mattered.

"Holding you felt good, Rachel. Good, and right."

She drew in a slow breath, held it for several moments. Then her lips curved into a smile that sent his stomach into a roll.

"Next time I cuddle up to you, cowboy, I'll make sure I'm awake."

A tightness he hadn't realized was banding his chest slipped a notch or two. Jake felt a grin start easy and spread slow.

"Next time we cuddle, sweetheart, I'll make sure you *stay* awake. For the first few hours, anyway."

Laughing at the cocky promise, she rose up on her toes, looped her arms around his neck, and claimed the kiss he was aching to give her.

Lord, she tasted fine! Clean and scrubbed from the icy water she'd bathed with this morning. Sunshiny and warm from standing in the dappled sunlight. The hunger Jake had beaten into submission in the early hours of the dawn clawed at him again. Only the thought that he'd have her alone for at least a day and another night while they chased down the source of the copper ore kept Jake from dragging her down to the springy, pine-carpeted forest floor.

The irony of the situation didn't escape him. He'd resisted the same savage urge at Three Rock Canyon in the noble belief that Rachel deserved better than bawling cows and rocks under her back. Now, she'd be lucky if they made it a mile or more from Grizzly's cabin before he claimed the gift she was offering in every eager move of her mouth under his. Before he could claim anything, though, he had to cut loose from Russ Taggart.

The cutting proved difficult. The FBI agent's eyes narrowed when Jake told him he intended to leave with Marsh and Shad after all.

"Why? I thought you wanted to keep an eye on things here."

"I've decided I've got better things to do."

"You know these mountains, Henderson. We could use your help tracking Grizzly's pet."

"Buck's one of the best trackers in the county. With him on your team, you don't need me." Securing his bedroll atop the ATV's carrier, Jake threw the agent a bone. "Marsh or I or one of my other brothers will guide the rest of your people up here when they assemble in Flagstaff. When does your team get in?"

"They'll be arriving at various times today. One of my men will contact me when they're ready to roll."

Taggart apparently didn't like the sudden change in plans. At all. Shifting his attention to the woman at Jake's side, he laid it on with a heavy hand.

"How about you, Rachel? You've been part of

this investigation from the beginning. Don't you want to stay to see it through?''

"You know I do. But I came to Flagstaff to take care of my aunt, remember? If I'm going to be away from her for any length of time, I need to make arrangements for someone to stay with her."

As excuses went, it was pretty weak. She could have entrusted the task of looking after Alice to Jake or Marsh or anyone else at the Bar-H.

"I'll see you tomorrow or the day after," she promised Taggart. "As soon as I get done what needs doing."

They traveled for a good twenty minutes. Jake waited until he was sure the echoes from the ATVs wouldn't carry back to the men above them before he slowed to a stop. Killing the engine, he swung off and walked back to the other two men.

"This is where we part company."

Marsh eyed him speculatively. "Going to do a little hunting on your own, bro?"

"Prospecting."

"Come again?"

Succinctly, Jake recounted Rachel's discovery of the copper sulfide nuggets in the grooves of Grizzly's boots.

"She thinks he might have stashed the money in the abandoned copper mine on the next ridge."

Marsh and Shad treated her to identical looks of skepticism.

"I know, I know. It's a long shot. I just want to check it out."

"So this is what you meant when you told your friend you had things that needed doing?"

Rachel lifted a shoulder. The fact that she'd "filtered" the truth again didn't appear to worry her unduly.

"Taggart's gonna bust a gut when he finds out you two went lookin' for his precious money on your own," Shad predicted.

"Not if we find it."

"That's a mighty big 'if,' missy."

"I know."

Tipping his hat over the bridge of his nose, the foreman scratched his head. "I'm thinking maybe we should ride along with you two."

Jake shook his head. Shad's glance drifted from him to Rachel and back again.

"Then again," he mused, "maybe not."

Swinging off his vehicle, Marsh unstrapped the extra fuel containers. "Odds are you're going off on a wild-goose chase, but we'll leave you our extra fuel and the food we packed in with us. Just in case you get lucky," he added with a bland look at his brother.

"Will you check on Alice for me when you get

down?'' Rachel asked after he'd transferred the fuel container, a dented coffeepot and a few cans. "Tell her I'm with Jake."

"Sure thing." Revving his ATV, the DEA agent offered a final piece of advice. "Forty million dollars is a good-sized chunk of change. Watch yourselves."

In her heart of hearts, Rachel suspected Marsh was right. The odds were they were off on a long, wild-goose chase. Yet a heady sense of adventure bubbled in her veins as she maneuvered her vehicle behind Jake's.

Adventure, and a wild, pulsing excitement. The last time she'd ridden off alone with this man, she'd done her darnedest to get him naked. This time, she had every intention of finishing the job. Her pulse accelerated each time she opened the throttles and fluttered with impatience whenever she slowed for a rough patch.

There were plenty of those. They had to cut down a steep slope, then back up before they reached the rim of the bluff. The pines thinned toward the top, their roots fighting for a hold in the striated rock. They navigated the bluff for three or four miles, then cut down another, almost perpendicular slope. At the bottom, they picked up a narrow dirt road that followed the course of a bubbling mountain stream.

Jake slowed, idling his ATV's engine while he waited for Rachel to pull alongside him. "This road leads up to the copper mine."

"How far is it?"

"Another five, six miles. We could make it before dark if we pushed. Or we could camp here."

Rachel rolled her head to ease her knotted neck muscles. "Five or six miles, huh?"

"I vote we camp here." A gleam came into his blue eyes. "I don't want to take a chance on tiring you completely out."

Hot, sweet anticipation flooded her veins and put a thread of throaty laughter in her reply.

"Neither do I."

Chapter 11

If Rachel was ever offered a vote on the matter, she would definitely opt for making slow, delicious love beside a bubbling mountain stream instead of a fast, furious tussle at the bottom of a rocky canyon.

When it came right down to it, she couldn't have imagined a more perfect setting. The sky glowing with the first, faint streaks of red. The sun sinking slowly and striking fiery sparks off the snow on the peaks. Air so clean and sharp it seared her lungs. And Jake...

Dear Lord, Jake...

He could have given lessons in tender. And

sweet. And maddening. He set the pace from the first, feeding her kisses while he set up a rudimentary camp, tantalizing her with brief tastes, refusing to be rushed.

"Not this time," he murmured against her mouth. "No grabbing for you at the bottom of a gully. No dust swirling around us or bawling calves as an audience. This time, there's only you and me, sweetheart."

She caught his face between her hands, feeling the whiskery abrasion of his cheeks, searching his eyes. No doubts lingered in their depths. No shadows masked a deep, hidden hurt. He was right, Rachel thought with a wild thump of her heart. There was only the two of them.

Absurdly, the realization filled her with shyness. After hungering for this man so intensely and waging a silent battle with his memories, she was suddenly unsure of what to do with the victory he handed her in every kiss.

As it turned out, she didn't have to do a thing. Zipping the two sleeping bags together, Jake arranged them into a soft, cushiony bed and laid her back. The flap of the bag covered him. His heat covered her.

He was so incredibly gentle, so incredibly skilled. His mouth molded hers with slow, drugging kisses. His hands roamed her throat, her shoulders, her breasts. He needed no help removing their outer layers of clothing, alternating her boots with his, sliding her jeans down her hips, her sweater over her head.

Cold air danced on her face and shoulder. Jake's hard, hot body burned on every other square inch of her skin. He held her mouth with his while his callused palm planed her waist and the flare of her hips, then traveled back up to her breast. Somehow, he managed to contort his body enough to take the aching nipple in his mouth. Rachel jumped at the scrape of his teeth against her engorged flesh.

"Jake..."

"Easy, sweetheart. We'll go easy."

Rachel soon discovered that his definition of easy differed considerably from her. When he gently kneed her legs apart, his hair-roughened thigh created a tormenting friction. That left her uneasy enough. Then his fingers slipped under her panties and found the tight nub of flesh at her center. After the first few strokes, Rachel's uncharacteristic passivity went up in a burst of heat.

One of her arms locked around his neck. Her legs tangled with his, trapping his wrist between her thighs, jamming his rigid shaft against her hip. It took a frantic wiggle or two, but Rachel managed to wedge a hand between their straining bodies, press her palm against the bulge and create a little friction of her own.

Jake's back and shoulder muscles went taut. She knew a moment of delicious triumph, then his gentleness disappeared and his mouth ravaged hers. She was gasping when he stripped off her panties, couldn't drag in so much as a single breath when he slid first one finger, then another into her hot, slick core. With a skill that left her moaning, he primed her, thrusting in, out, in again.

She was wet and hot and aching when he withdrew his hand and eased away. He rolled onto his side, his back to her, his shoulders hunched. Rachel swallowed another groan, this one of sheer dismay. Oh, no! Not again! Surely he wasn't having second thoughts!

Her breath ragged, she propped herself up on one elbow. A dozen different protests tumbled through her head. Then he reached for his jeans and extracted a condom from his wallet and she let out a fluttery sigh of relief. In her mounting passion, she'd forgotten about Jake's inbred sense of responsibility and need to protect.

His shoulder muscles rippled as he sheathed himself, and the most idiotic warmth flowered in Rachel's chest. She was a grown woman, for heaven's sake. An adult both capable of and used to taking care of herself. A professional prepared to stand by her analyses and take the heat, if necessary. Yet the idea of letting Jake protect her stirred some deep, primitive sense of feminine satisfaction.

She nibbled on her lower lip, more than a little embarrassed by the feeling. It certainly wasn't one she'd admit to among her circle of professional contacts. Maybe she was just out of her element and recognized it, she rationalized. Overwhelmed by all these rugged mountains, tall, swaying pines and swooping hawks. She was experiencing nature at its most majestic, most elemental. Maybe she'd just gotten caught up in the place and the circumstances.

The thought absorbed her until Jake rolled back, and she knew what she was feeling didn't have diddly to do with mountains or pine trees. Gulping, she took in his wide, muscled shoulders. The sweat glistening on his chest. The rigid shaft thrusting up from its nest of dark, wiry hair.

But it was his smile that turned her insides to a quivering mélange of mush. Half tender, half pure, hungry male, it was all Jake.

"Still awake?"

All hungry female, she nodded. "Wide awake."

"Good." His smile feathered into a wicked grin as he drew her under him. "Let's see if we can keep you that way for those hours I promised you."

Her stomach quivered as he positioned himself between her thighs. The first thrust was agonizingly slow, the withdrawal even slower. The second went a little harder, a little deeper. Rachel lost count after the third or fourth stroke. By then, her tongue had found his, her back was arched, and her fingers were digging into his taut, tight rear in an effort to hurry things along.

He wouldn't be hurried, dammit!

"Jake!"

"Not yet." Every sinew and tendon in his body corded, he drew back. "Not yet, Rachel. I want to..."

He snapped his jaw shut, his entire body resisting the pull of her eager muscles. Some hazy corner of her mind sensed that he was holding back to make sure he didn't take his own release at the expense of hers. Unfortunately—or fortunately!—Rachel had passed the point of holding back. Hooking her legs around his thighs, she slammed her hips into his.

A groan rumbled up from his chest. He surged into her, full and heavy and bone-hard. Her lips parted on a gurgle that might have been triumph or relief or pleasure. Whatever it was, it got lost in another gasp as her womb clenched around him. When the first tight swirls began, she squeezed her eyes shut and threw back her head. Within moments, the white-hot sensations were piling one on top of the other.

She rode the crest, her back arched, her body shuddering. Pleasure splintered through her. The spiraling waves lifted her, carried her, crashed down on her.

Only after she lay boneless and breathless did Jake take his own release. Fisting his hands in her hair, he thrust into her once, twice, again. Suddenly, his body went rigid. Burying his face in her hair, he followed her over the edge.

Still shuddering, Rachel burrowed her nose in the warm, damp flesh of his neck. Slowly, the world righted itself. The fleeting notion entered her head that finding the missing forty million dollars might constitute a definite and distinct anticlimax.

With their basic, most urgent need satisfied, they attended to more mundane matters such as food and fire.

More used to participating than spectating, Rachel felt guilty about lying limp and languid in the warmth of their zipped-together sleeping bag while Jake dragged on his clothes and took care of the housekeeping chores. Not, however, guilty enough to extend more than a token offer of assistance.

"You stay warm," he replied, smiling as he took in her tousled hair and obvious disinclination to move. "I think I can handle this."

There was no thinking about it. The man certainly knew his way around the great outdoors. Snuggling down in her warm cocoon, Rachel could only admire his smooth efficiency as he started a small, snapping fire, then dug around in his ATV's carrier for a fishing line. Her interest took a slight dip when he baited the line with something white and squiggly he dug from under a rotting log.

Yech! Profoundly relieved that he'd volunteered to handle matters without involving her, she dragged the flap of the sleeping bag up to her nose. Warm and comfortable, she watched while he selected a large, flat rock in midstream. Rachel had no idea whether fish would rise to the bait this late in the day, but had to admit she enjoyed the sight of Jake hunkered down and waiting with seemingly endless patience.

She must have dozed off, because the next thing she knew Jake was kneeling beside the stream, cleaning his catch. His movements economical and sure, he gutted the speckled trout and spitted it on a forked branch. Moments later, he propped the trout over the crackling, popping campfire. Water from the stream was already boiling in the dented tin coffeepot Marsh had contributed, to which Jake added a handful of unground beans.

Her now rumbling stomach gave a joyful leap when he lined up a couple of cans and opened them with the tool on his pocketknife. With silent thanks to Marsh for donating the extra food supplies, she dragged on her sweater and tucked the sleeping bag around her waist.

Her mouth was soon watering at the aromas that drifted her way. Still comfortably ensconced in the sleeping bag, she dined al fresco on the crusty trout and beans Jake served her, washed down with a mug of hot coffee. A dessert of canned peaches followed.

"I could get used to service like this," she said, licking sticky sweet syrup from her fingers. "I'm trying to remember the last time I had dinner in bed. It was, umm, never."

"Really?" He hooked his boots at the ankles and stretched out on his half of the rumpled sleeping bag. "You've been missing out on one of the finer pleasures in life, woman. Ellen and I used to..."

He broke off, his face clouding. "Oh, hell. I'm sorry, Rachel."

"It's all right."

It *was* all right. Mostly. But she could see he needed convincing.

"Ellen was part of your life. Part of you, Jake. Everything you two shared made you into the man you are today. And I... I like the man you are."

It was too soon to talk of love. Neither one of them was ready, despite their acrobatics a while ago and the musky scent that still clung to their skin.

"I remember meeting Ellen, but never got to know her very well. Will you tell me about her?"

"No."

The quiet refusal hit Rachel like a slap in the face. She jerked her chin up, stung. Jake caught the movement, swore, and apologized again.

"I'm sorry. I didn't mean it like that."

"Maybe you'd better tell me how you did mean it," she said carefully.

"This is our time. Our night, Rachel. The reference to Ellen just slipped out. I wasn't thinking about her."

His hand came up and tucked a tangled strand of hair behind Rachel's ear.

"I was thinking about you, sweetheart, and about how much I'd like to deliver a whole lot more meals to your bed."

She wanted to believe him. With a need so fierce it stunned her, Rachel wanted desperately to believe him.

He must have read the need in her eyes. Sliding his hand around her nape, he drew her closer and rested his forehead against hers.

"I've never made love beside a mountain stream like this, with the wind crying through the trees and the taste of peaches and a wild, sweet woman in my mouth."

Rachel understood instantly what he was doing.

He was stamping this night, this place, as theirs and theirs alone. A shudder of delight rippled down her spine.

"Cold?"

"A little."

"This room service comes with more than just roasted trout and peaches." With a smooth, sure tug, he drew her into his lap. "Want me to get you warm and toasty again before you zonk out for the night?"

"Sounds like a plan to me, cowboy."

She managed to hold on for another couple of hours before she fulfilled Jake's prediction and crashed for the night. They were, she decided just before she gave herself up to total oblivion, quality hours.

From his concealed position some two hundred yards away, Russ Taggart steadied his blue-steel automatic on a tumbled boulder and sighted through the infrared targeting system. The grip was cold and smooth in his hand. His thumb itched to flick the lever and paint a tiny red target on one of the dim shapes humped inside the sleeping bag.

They were too far away for him to make out their features, but he'd seen enough to guess that Henderson's expression would have gone slack with satisfaction and Rachel's heavy with sleep. God, they'd been wrestling inside that damned bag for over an hour, since before Russ spotted their campfire and moved in as close as he dared.

Anger knotted his insides. At Henderson, for going off on his own hunt like this. At Rachel, for going with him. He'd half expected it of Henderson. He'd spent too many years in the Bureau to believe any man would pass up the chance at forty million dollars.

What he hadn't expected was Rachel Quinn's defection to the enemy. Russ had trusted her. He'd used her for his own purposes, sure, but he'd respected and trusted her. At least until she'd started letting her hots for Henderson get in the way of her judgment. Did she think the rancher was going to cut her in on the money if they found it? More to the point, did she imagine Russ would let him?

His finger caressed the trigger. He could take them out right there, right where they lay. They wouldn't know what hit them. He'd have hell to pay justifying it, particularly to Henderson's brothers. Russ could do it, though. If he could convince that hick deputy sheriff to sit on his hands and wait for the rest of his team to arrive while Russ did some looking around on his own, he could rationalize the death of these two fortune hunters.

The lure of those lost millions had sucked them in. They'd set out on their own, caught him tracking them. Henderson had whipped out his high-powered rifle. Russ had tried to reason with him, tried to get him to see he couldn't keep any of that money, had fired only to defend himself. Tragically, Rachel had gone down in the exchange.

It would be messy. Russ would have to reposition the bodies to explain the angle of fire. He'd probably be put on administrative leave while an independent investigator determined whether the circumstances warranted the use of deadly force. But he'd worked enough crime scenes to make the deaths appear justifiable.

He didn't take either Henderson or Rachel out, though. As much as he despised her for going over to the enemy, he needed her. Needed Henderson, too. At least until they got wherever they were going. They had a specific destination in mind. They wouldn't have parted company with Henderson's brother and taken off on their own unless...

Unless Jake Henderson couldn't wait to get the bitch to himself and jump her bones.

For a moment, doubt sliced into Taggart's gut. He lowered the automatic, his hand fisted around the cross-hatching on the grip.

No. That wasn't it. Henderson could have taken her to a nice, warm hotel room in Flagstaff if he didn't want to do her at the ranch, with all his relatives listening to the bedsprings rattle. There was more to this detour into the mountains than mere lust.

There had to be.

Sliding his back down the rock behind him, he settled in to wait for the dawn.

Chapter 12

The tantalizing aroma of coffee dragged Rachel from sleep. Prying open one lid, she eyed the mug weaving a lazy figure eight under her nose.

"Whatimeizit?"

A hint of laughter threaded through the low, rumbling reply. "Approximately twenty-five and a half hours later than the last time you asked me that question."

That was too much for her still-fuzzy mind. Poking her head out of the sleeping bag's swaddling folds, she squinted through heavy lids.

"Huh?"

Jake knelt in front of her. Whiskers darkened his

cheeks and chin, which no doubt accounted for the slight burning sensation on Rachel's own cheek when she attempted a weak smile.

"You want to run that by me again? I'm, uh, not at my best in the morning."

"It's just past seven," he said, graciously ignoring her statement of the obvious. "Here's your coffee. Hope you don't mind warmed-over beans for breakfast?"

Actually, Rachel couldn't think of anything less appetizing at the moment. The closest she usually came to breakfast was a bagel slathered with cream cheese around nine or ten o'clock, and then only when she didn't have a lunch scheduled.

"Coffee's all I need," she murmured, burying her nose in the mug he handed her.

"You sure?"

"Mmm."

"I'll pack up and refuel the vehicles, then."

He moved away with his easy stride, leaving Rachel to unfuzz her mind. The coffee helped. Thick and hickory-flavored, it left a bitter taste as it went down, but provided enough of a jolt to stir her sluggish brain cells. Enough to notice how good Jake looked in the morning, anyway.

Despite the sandpapery whiskers…or maybe because of them…he seemed to fit right in with his surroundings. His faded blue flannel shirt owed nothing to high-priced designers. His vest with its warm, curly-haired lining might have come from one of the mountain sheep that bounded through the Rockies. Under the brim of his hat, his eyes were the same color as the sky collecting light from the sun still hidden behind the eastern peaks. He must have cleaned up in the stream while she slept, because the hair that showed under his hat carried a damp gleam.

Rachel, on the other hand, knew she must look as frowsy and frumpled as she felt. She rarely bothered with much makeup, but after two days in the mountains she would have forked over a good portion of her next month's paycheck for a few essential cosmetics.

She would have paid even more for toiletries. All she carried with her besides the wet wipes and sunblock Lauren had stuck in the ATV carrier was the bar of soap Shad had appropriated from his cousin's cabin yesterday morning. She'd used the wet wipes to scrub both her face and her teeth. They had done the job, but didn't provide quite the same level of confidence as a toothbrush and dental floss.

Grimacing, Rachel set the coffee mug aside. She'd better find a private bend of the stream and get to work. With a little grunt, she wriggled into her clothes. Her hours on the ATV yesterday had generated an assortment of aching muscles. The hours she'd spent with Jake last night seemed to have generated a few more.

She slanted him a considering glance as she tugged on her socks and boots, wondering whether he felt any unaccustomed aches…and what he thought about them if he did. Now that her mind was semifunctional again, she also registered the fact that he hadn't touched her this morning or made any reference to their explosive, exhausting lovemaking last night. Neither had she, of course, but still….

Maybe he wasn't a morning person either, she thought, tugging at her bootlaces. Maybe he just needed a little encouragement. Next time, she would agree to beans for breakfast, let him serve her in bed, and see what happened.

If there was a next time.

Jake's gruff assertion that last night was their special time floated through her mind. Frowning, she flicked him another glance. His words had snared her attention at the time. This morning, they started a queer little sensation curling in her chest.

Rachel returned to the campsite some twenty minutes later. The cold water, soap, and wet wipes had worked minor miracles. She felt close to human again, and confident enough to make the first move.

Dropping her few toiletries in the ATV carrier,

she crossed to the other vehicle. Jake leaned against its seat, his long legs crossed at the ankle, his eyes on the slopes above and behind them.

"Sorry I'm such a slow starter."

When he didn't respond, the smile she'd sent his way slipped a notch.

"Jake?"

"Sorry. What did you say?"

"I said I was sorry you had to pack everything up. I usually pull my share of the load."

"No problem." He aimed another glance at the slopes. "Are you ready to roll?"

Rachel drew in a sharp breath. She wasn't looking for morning-after assurances or pledges of undying devotion, but a friendly smile or two didn't seem too much to hope for.

"No," she answered slowly. "I'm not ready to roll. What's going on here?"

His gaze cut back to her. "What do you mean?"

His closed, wary expression hurt. More than Rachel had thought possible. The Jake she'd wrestled with in the sleeping bag yesterday afternoon was gone.

"Why are you so...?" She waved a hand in small circles. "So distracted?"

"I thought I saw something moving up in those rocks. It was probably a mountain sheep, or maybe a cougar. They like to hunt early in the mornings."

The idea of a mountain lion prowling around in the immediate vicinity was daunting enough without Jake taking her elbow to steer her toward her vehicle and suggesting briskly that she mount up.

Rachel dug in her heels. "Hold on a moment. Is that all that's bothering you this morning? Are you sure it's not us? Or more specifically, what happened between us last night? Do you want to talk about it?"

"Does it need talking about?"

"Yes. No. Not really."

Exasperated at her less than articulate response, Rachel raked her fingers through her hair.

"It's just that a woman generally expects more than a cup of coffee and an order to mount up and move out in the morning. At least, this woman does."

He managed to look wounded and amused at the same time. "And here I thought I was being such a gentleman for not forcing my attentions on someone who pointedly informed me she isn't at her best in the mornings."

"Yes, well, I just needed a little time to get my motor revved."

"Is it going now?"

"The throttle's wide open."

"Good."

Planting his hands on her waist, he swept her

forward. The kiss he laid on her lips wasn't the least friendly or gentle or good morning-ish. It was as fierce as the sun, as hard and rough as the mountains.

"Now that," Rachel told him when she came up for air, "was worth waking up for."

So was the grin he aimed her way as he hustled her toward her vehicle. "Let's get this show on the road. Not that I expect to find anything at this abandoned mine of yours, you understand. But the sooner we check it out, the sooner we can get you back down to civilization."

"Just me? What about you, Jake?"

"I was thinking I might head back up to check on your friend Taggart, but…"

"But?" she prompted, curious about what was going on his head concerning Russ's investigation. Whatever it was, he kept it to himself.

"But after last night," he said, diverting her with a wolfish grin, "I'm developing a yen to see what it would feel like to share a real mattress with you."

"A yen?"

"Okay, a craving."

More than satisfied with his admission, Rachel climbed onto her four-wheeler. With a last look over his shoulder at the rocks behind them, Jake did the same.

* * *

The road leading to the mine had fallen into total disrepair. They had to skirt tumbled boulders and potholes the size of lunar craters but reached the abandoned site a little over an hour later.

Chewing on her lower lip, Rachel slowed her vehicle to a stop and killed the engine. When she surveyed the tumbled-down buildings and boarded-up entrance to the mine, ramshackle was the word that came immediately to mind. Dangerous followed closely on its heels.

With a background in materials science, Rachel had a good idea what to expect inside. There was no easy way to extract copper from the earth, although it had been mined almost since the dawn of time.

Functional as well as beautiful, the mineral served a host of purposes. Ancient Egyptians had discovered its ductility and used copper to line pipes carrying water from the Nile. Because of its resistance to corrosion, Greek and Roman architects had sheathed their roofs and columns in copper sheeting. In modern times, the mineral's electrical conductivity generated huge demands. Millions of tons of copper went into electrical wires and circuit boards each year.

Most of the copper mined today in the U.S. came from Arizona. Low-grade ore was dug out of open pits. Higher grade sulfides, like the nuggets Rachel had found embedded in Grizzly's boot, had to be mined by means of a shaft sunk deep in the earth's surface or by tunneling into the side of a mountain.

This was one of those horizontal tunnels, referred to in mining parlance as an adit. From the main passageway, the miners would have dug numerous side tunnels. There were probably dozens of those suckers, Rachel thought with a sinking feeling. The idea of spending several hours poking around in small, dark passageways was losing more of its appeal with each passing moment.

It lost even more when Jake unlatched the plastic scabbard attached to his ATV and extracted his rifle. Calmly, he checked the chamber and reset the safety, then slung the weapon over one shoulder.

"Just a little insurance," he said, catching her look.

Shad's assertion that mountain cats, bears and skunks inhabited most of the caves and hidey-holes in these mountains came rushing back. Rachel sincerely hoped Grizzly's pet or one of his relatives hadn't taken up residence in the abandoned mine.

"These mines usually have several airshafts, as well as second or third entrances. No telling what kind of creatures we might meet on the way in."

"Oh, that's comforting."

"Or on the way out," he murmured, slipping a box of bullets into his vest pocket.

Before Rachel could ask him just what specific creatures he had in mind, he went to work on the rotting boards blocking the entrance. Their rusted nails gave with only a small shriek or two of protest. Jake pried loose three boards and set them to one side.

"Hope the batteries in this flashlight are still good," he muttered.

He worked the button, and light stabbed the darkness inside the tunnel. Bending, he stepped over the remaining boards and disappeared.

Well, they'd come this far, Rachel thought as she crawled through the opening after him. They might as well see what they could find inside.

The first thing that hit her was the cold. The second was the stink. The dank air carried a dozen different smells, none of them pleasant. Iron tracks and old equipment lay corroding in the darkness. The beams supporting the tunnel roof gave off the decaying odor of wood rot. Piles of animal droppings added their own stench. Some, she noted with a gulp, appeared relatively fresh. Careful where she set her feet, she followed the stabbing beam of Jake's flashlight into the darkness.

Rachel could never decide afterward who was more surprised when they stumbled on the money, she or Jake.

He was in the lead, probing the darkness with his flashlight as they explored one of the side tunnels. They'd gone about twenty or thirty yards in when the beam skipped right over the neatly stacked bricks. With a startled oath, Jake brought it stabbing back.

"Well, I'll be damned!"

The long empty tunnel amplified his exclamation and sent it booming down the passageway. Almost dancing with excitement, Rachel added to the reverberating echoes.

"I don't believe it! We found it, Jake! We actually found the missing shipment!"

"That's what it looks like."

Brushing past him, she dropped to her knees to examine the banding on the bricks. Each was stamped with the seal of the U.S. Bureau of Engraving and Printing. It took only a glance at the serial number on the top bills to identify them as from the missing shipment.

"Taggart's going to stroke out!" she declared. "He's become obsessed with wrapping this case up."

"I noticed."

Still on a high, she ignored the dry response. "We've got to get word to him. The walkie-talkies in the ATV don't have enough range. We'll have to head back to the line shack, or find the nearest phone.''

''My guess is he'll find us soon enough.''

The drawled comment brought her head up with a snap. ''Find us?''

''He's following us.''

''Russ?''

''Russ. I wasn't sure this morning, when I spotted that movement in the rocks. I'd asked Buck Silverthorne to keep an eye on him, for one thing. For another, I couldn't understand how he knew where we were heading. I figured it out during the ride up to the mine.''

She couldn't see his eyes in the darkness, but the coolness that seeped into his voice started a prickling at the back of her neck.

''Suppose you tell me just what you figured out.''

''One of us must have tipped him off.''

She went still. Utterly still. Ice crystals formed in her veins.

''That one being…?''

His shrug cut into her heart like the hunting knife he'd used to clean the trout last night. Jake still thought she was setting him up.

Furious denials rose in her chest. Anger piled swift and high on top of her hurt. Clamping her lips together, Rachel refused to let either spill out. She'd groveled as much as she intended to, and the realization that Jake didn't trust her after what they'd shared last night hurt so badly she could hardly speak.

"You think...?" She swallowed the lump that had lodged in her throat. "You think I told Russ about the mine?"

"Maybe not in so many words, but..."

She couldn't hold her pain back. It was too sharp, and her anger too hot.

"Go to hell."

"What?"

"Go to straight to hell, Henderson. Do not pass go. Do not collect two hundred dollars on the way. And do *not* speak to me again, ever!"

In a more rational moment, Rachel would have recognized that last bit for the childishness it was. She wasn't feeling anything close to rational at the moment, however. As furious with herself for hurting so much as she was with him, she whirled and stomped toward the main passageway.

Cursing, Jake started after her. He'd bungled that, and badly. He hadn't intended his suppositions as accusations. He could only lay his clumsiness on the shock of actually finding the damned money and the unease that had nagged him since he'd spotted that movement up in the rocks.

He caught up with her in the main tunnel and

snagged her arm. "Rachel, listen to me. I don't think you tipped Taggart off intentionally. Maybe it was something in your face when you pulled me aside yesterday morning, or something you let drop when you were working in the cabin."

"Well, that's a relief," she said scathingly. "You just think I'm stupid. For a moment there, I had the impression you thought Russ and I had planned this, and that I let you crawl into my sleeping bag just to get you to lead us to the mine."

"Dammit! How could you jump to a conclusion like that?"

"Oh, I don't know. Maybe because you jumped to the conclusion that I clued Taggart in, intentionally or otherwise. Just out of curiosity, why the hell didn't you tell me he followed us?"

"I wasn't sure at first and didn't want to worry you unnecessarily."

"You didn't want to worry me?" Her voice shot up a full octave. "You didn't want to worry me!"

"All right, maybe that was a mistake."

"No kidding! Listen to me, Henderson." Yanking her arm free, she stabbed a forefinger into his chest to emphasize her points. "One, I don't need protecting. I admit I liked the dinner in bed bit, but when it comes right down to it, I can get my own damned dinner. Two, I didn't tip Taggart off. Three, if he *is* following us, we tell him about the money,

I go back to D.C., you go back to being a jerk, and this whole mess is over with.''

"I'm afraid it's not quite over, Rache.''

The voice came out of the darkness behind them. With another savage oath, Jake spun around. When a streak of red light lasered through the tunnel and centered on Rachel's right breast, the suspicions that had nagged at him for the past few days coalesced into dead certainty.

Chapter 13

Stunned, Rachel searched the murky darkness for the man behind the weapon aimed at her heart.

"Russ?"

He stepped into the flashlight's beam. He held his automatic two-fisted and chest high. "Yeah, it's me."

"What in *hell* are you doing?"

"Closing this investigation, just like you said. No, Henderson, don't move! I can pump a bullet into both you and Rachel a whole lot faster than you can get your weapon off your shoulder. In fact, I think you should lay it down, nice and slow."

The flashlight's beam jerked, as if Jake's fist had

tightened around the shaft. Taggart's chuckle drifted down the dank, fetid passageway.

"You can kill your light if you want to, Henderson, but I suspect you realize this infrared targeting scope illuminates both of you like a spotlight. Put the rifle down. Now."

Slowly, Jake bent and deposited his rifle. It hit bedrock with a small thunk.

Still targeted with a small red dot, Rachel burst out, "You're reading this all wrong, Russ! We didn't come looking for your precious millions with the intention of ripping them off."

"I think he knows that."

Jake's drawl drew another chuckle from Taggart. "Figured it out, have you, Henderson?"

"Figured *what* out?" Rachel demanded for the second time in a totally confusing ten minutes.

"Your friend's not after the money," Jake said softly. "Not anymore, anyway. Now, his main concern is making sure it doesn't track back to him."

"To him?"

Her jaw sagging in disbelief, Rachel swung her gaze from the man illuminated in the flashlight's beam to the one standing taut and tense beside her.

"That's crazy! Russ has been on this case like a bulldog on a T-bone since the day he was appointed to the accident investigation task force."

"My guess is that he was working the accident

well before he was appointed…or arranged to be appointed to the task force. How long did it take you to set up the drop, Taggart? Six months? A year?''

''Almost three years, actually. The toughest part was accessing the codes that locked the transport containers in place aboard the aircraft. The Bureau of Engraving and Printing doesn't particularly like to share that information. Once I knew how to get at the codes, I had to find someone willing to blow the cargo hatch in midflight and eject the container.''

Rachel couldn't believe what she was hearing. She hadn't always agreed with Taggart during their months on the task force, had fought him tooth and nail on several key issues, but the idea he'd engineered the accident they'd both spent so many months investigating sickened her.

''Why?'' Still struggling to understand, she demanded an explanation. ''Why in God's name would you send four men to their deaths?''

''The crash wasn't part of the plan,'' he snapped, losing some of his cool composure. ''DC-10's have sprung cargo hatches before and made safe landings. I'm not responsible for the damned blizzard.''

''You still haven't answered my question. Why, Russ?''

''You're a civil servant,'' he sneered. ''Just like

me. You know how much we make. Forty million was too tempting to resist. So was the challenge of grabbing it right out from under the nose of the Secret Service.''

Rachel couldn't care less about the long-standing rivalries between the Secret Service, a division of the U.S. Department of Treasury, and the other law enforcement communities.

''We've alerted every bank in the country to watch for these bills,'' she reminded the FBI agent grimly. ''You can't spend them.''

''Now I can't. But eight or ten years from now...''

Fury surged into her as she finally understood his intent. ''Oh, I get it. You intended to sit on the money until the statute of limitations ran out, then launder it through an off-shore bank.''

''That was the plan.''

Cold and icy calm, Jake's voice floated to her through the darkness. ''The plan went down the tubes when bills started popping up around Flag-staff, didn't it, Taggart? It was only a matter of time until the bills and container were found.''

Rachel's breath hissed out. ''The container! We speculated it was fitted with some kind of signaling or tracking device so it could be found after it hit the ground.''

It would have required sophisticated electronics.

With components that could be traced back to their purchaser.

"That's what you're really after, isn't it, Russ? The container?"

"You got it, kid. I built that signaling device by hand. I was careful, very careful, but I can't take the chance of letting it fall into the wrong hands. Old man McCoy couldn't have carted all these bricks far. Now that I know their location, I can concentrate my search for the container in the immediate area and let the rest of my team scatter to hell and back. Too bad you won't be part of the search effort, Rache. We made a good team."

His false air of regret sickened her almost as much as the certainty of what would come next. Instinctively, she edged closer to Jake.

"Don't lay any compliments on me, you bastard. I don't want them from you. I don't want anything from you, except to watch Buck Silverthorne cart you off wearing your own cuffs."

"That's not going to happen. Move away from Henderson, Rachel, and walk toward me."

She choked down the panic that rose like bile in her throat. "Get stuffed!"

"I'll shoot you both where you stand if I have to. The explanations would be messy, but I can work it. I'd rather make it look natural. Move away from him."

"Do as he says, Rachel."

Jake reached over with his free hand and squeezed her arm before pushing her aside. With his other, he kept the flashlight beam trained on Taggart. Rachel forced herself forward, cursing her one-time partner with every dragging step.

She knew Jake wouldn't move as long as Russ had her targeted. He wouldn't risk her life, but he'd risk his own. Terror churning in her stomach, she formulated a desperate plan. She'd throw herself forward. Fall on the gun. Take Taggart's arm down with her. Give Jake time to lunge.

Every nerve in her body screaming, she coiled her muscles. Suddenly, Taggart surged forward. His fist came out of the darkness, cut through the beam of white light, and slammed into her jaw.

Rachel sank without a sound. She was still on her way down when Jake launched himself through the air.

The FBI operative's years of training and experience had him anticipating just such an attack. Flinging up an arm, he took the flashlight with a crack of metal on bone. His other arm whipped around.

Jake crashed into him at the same instant the automatic's blue-steel handle smashed into his skull. Blinding white pain exploding in his head, he took Taggart down.

They hit with a force that knocked grunts from both men. Locked together, they grappled in the darkness. Swearing, straining, struggling frantically, Taggart used every move in his bag of dirty tricks.

Jake had survived his share of barroom brawls, both before and during his stint in the marines. He and his brothers had invented a few tricks of their own during their rambunctious youth. Ramming a knee into Taggart's gut, he followed with a hard right to the jaw and grabbed for the man's gun arm.

If the darkness and the searing pain in his temple hadn't blinded him, he might have gotten a better hold. With a snarl, Taggart ripped his arm free and brought the gun down again butt-first.

A muted roar pierced Rachel's stupor. She opened her eyes to complete darkness. She turned her head, groaning when the movement started waves of pain in her lower face.

It took her a few moments to realize that the darkness wasn't total. There, in the distance, was a dim grayness. Frowning, she stared at the faint coloration until it took shape. An oval. Half an oval.

The half made no sense to her. Frowning, she blinked to clear her confusion. It came back to her then, in a swift, terrifying rush. She was in a tunnel. That gray patch formed its entrance.

Jake! Dear God, where was Jake?

Ignoring the throbbing pain in her jaw, she crawled up on all fours and croaked out a hoarse cry.

"Jake?"

When she received no reply, panic rushed through her veins. Frantic, she scrabbled forward, rammed into something, and almost pitched over. The something, she discovered with a sob, was an inert body.

Only after her trembling hands encountered buttery soft sheepskin and burrowed under the curly lining to the chest beneath did she confirm that the body belonged to Jake. And that he was still breathing.

Sobbing with relief, she conducted another frantic, fumbling search. She found no bullet holes pumping hot, sticky blood.

His scalp was a mess, though. Plenty of blood there. Cradling him gently in her arms, Rachel sank back on her heels. Wave after wave of delayed shock shuddered through her.

She was still rocking Jake in her arms when the muted roar that had pulled her into consciousness penetrated her whirling mind once more. She craned her neck, frowning as the sound grew louder. Deep-throated echoes thundered through the tunnel.

Russ! It had to be Russ! On one of the four-wheelers. Was he coming back to look for them? He had to know the ATV wouldn't fit into this side tunnel.

Maybe it was Marsh, Rachel thought on a leap of desperate hope. Or Shad. Or Buck Silverthorne. She was still trying to decide what to do if it wasn't one of the good guys when the pale gray oval suddenly disappeared. A moment later, the deafening roar died.

For God's sake! What had Russ done? Blocked the tunnel entrance with the ATVs?

Did he think that would keep her and Jake inside? The scheme made no sense, until she remembered that he'd said he wanted to make things look natural. The pieces of the puzzle tumbled together with horrifying clarity.

What was more natural than burying her and Jake *and* the money they'd so foolishly gone looking for under tons of rock? It would take searchers days to find their bodies, dig them out. Days that Russ needed to look for his damned container.

And unless the bastard had packed some plastic explosive or dynamite along with him, the only means he had of creating an explosion was to put a bullet through the gas tank on one of the ATVs!

Terror came clawing back. One shot! That's all it would take. One shot from a safe distance down the main passageway. Scrambling back onto her knees, she threw her arm across Jake's chest and shook him.

"Jake! Wake up! We've got to move back, further down the tunnel!"

A groan rumbled from deep in his chest.

"Please, Jake. *Please!*"

She couldn't wait for him to come to. Her throat clogged with suffocating fear, Rachel scooted around and hooked her hands under his arms. Knees bent, back straining, she dragged his deadweight down the narrow tunnel.

Her hip slammed into rock. Her stumbling boot landed in something foul-smelling. Sweat popped out on her forehead, between her breasts.

How far had she gone? Twenty yards? Thirty? Not far enough! She was in total darkness now, her breath ragged and sharp. Thunder roared in her ears.

Five yards more. Ten. Dear God, she had to...

The bright flash when the ATV exploded was her only warning. Shock waves cannonaded down the tunnel, hammered at her eardrums, deafened her.

The ground beneath her feet trembled. The mountain shifted around her. The shriek of rock tearing away from rock pierced the ringing in Rachel's ears.

With a sobbing cry, she threw herself over Jake's body.

Chapter 14

"Jake?"

Her voice sounded tinny. Thin. Distant.

Rachel swiped her forearm across her face. The dust floating through the thick, pitch-black air burned her eyes and clogged her lungs. Her ears buzzed from the explosion's percussive blast. Her chin felt as though she'd connected with an iron horseshoe that was still attached to the horse. Her back, arms and legs ached from dragging Jake.

None of those minor pains took the edge from her singing, searing joy. The mountain hadn't fallen down on their heads! She and Jake were still alive!

For the time being, anyway.

That thought sobered her considerably. Crabbing sideways, Rachel scooted off Jake's chest. Still on all fours, she shook her head in a vain attempt to clear the ringing in her ears. All she succeeded in doing was making herself dizzy. Gulping, she forced back the nausea that rose in her throat.

Okay. All right. She needed to think, to analyze the situation. First, though, she had to gather enough data to determine just what the situation was!

Pushing to her feet, Rachel braced herself against the tunnel wall with a hand on either side. The rock felt icy cold under her fingers, but blessedly solid. Inch by cautious inch, she followed the wall back the way she'd come just frantic moments before.

She counted her steps, searching the darkness, afraid she'd see a shadowy form moving toward her, worried she'd see nothing at all. The foul-smelling mess she'd stepped in earlier told her she was getting close. She had reached step number fifty-three when she spotted a dim glow directly ahead.

Back to the wall, Rachel froze. It was Taggart. It had to be Taggart. His first attempt at burying her and Jake alive hadn't worked, so he'd come back for another try. Her heart in her throat, she stared at the light, waiting for it to move closer, praying it wouldn't, trying to work out her best plan of attack if it did.

Finally, her frantic mind absorbed the fact that the light was remaining stationary. She waited another two minutes. Three. A thousand, it seemed, before she inched forward again, even more cautiously than before.

The glow sharpened, brightened, resolved into a beam. With a muffled exclamation, Rachel skittered forward and scooped up the flashlight Jake must have dropped during the struggle. Whirling, she swept the beam back and forth across the tunnel floor.

"Yes!"

Almost tripping in giddy relief, she bent down and retrieved Jake's rifle. The odds were a little better now, she thought exultantly.

Her pumping excitement faded the moment she swung the flashlight toward the tunnel entrance. More correctly, where the entrance used to be. Tumbled slabs of rock the size of small trucks now blocked the passageway. She was still staring at them in blank dismay when a faint tapping came through the cracks.

"Rachel?"

Taggart's voice drifted to her, muted by the dust still sifting through the air. Like a small animal hiding from a predator, Rachel didn't move, didn't breathe. She wasn't about to alert Taggart to the fact that they were still alive and possibly trigger another explosion.

"Henderson?"

She heard a clatter of stone on stone, the scrabble of boots on loose rock. Still she didn't move.

Something fell, hit hard. Taggart cursed again. Footsteps thudded on the far side of the rock wall. He was moving away.

Swallowing, Rachel counted each muted tread, just as she'd counted her own just moments ago. He had to have reached the main passageway. Was he leaving the mine? Would he come back?

She had no idea how long she listened, every sense straining. Ten minutes? Twenty? It felt like hours. She was still locked in place, her nerves screaming with tension, when the sound of running footsteps behind her spun Rachel around.

Jake raced toward her, his expression murderous. Blood from the lacerations on his temple streaked one side of his face. Glistening red splotches stained his shirt and sheepskin vest.

"Rachel!"

"Shh!" She accompanied the fierce shush with a whispered order to keep his voice down. "I heard Taggart moving around a little while ago. I think he's left, but he may come back."

"You'd better give me the rifle."

"Take it." She was more than happy to surrender the lethal weapon. "I don't think it'll be much use, though. Not with *that* between you and your target."

Her hand wobbling, she aimed the flashlight at the tumbled wall of rock. Jake stared at it in blank astonishment.

"What the hell happened?"

"We had a slight explosion while you, uh, were sleeping."

Beneath the streaks of red, his eyes narrowed. "Are you okay?"

"Aside from an incipient bout of hysteria, I think so."

Evidently he disagreed with her self-diagnosis. Wrapping his fingers around her upper arm, he walked her over to the tumbled boulders.

"Sit down, put your head between your knees and breathe deeply."

"I'm okay. Really. Or I will be, when the buzzing in my ears goes away."

"Sit down."

Rachel sat. At that point she discovered she was shaking from head to foot.

"Tell me what happened," Jake ordered.

In short, succinct sentences, she told him.

Jake listened in silence. His jaw got tight when she described seeing the ATV blocking the entrance, even tighter when she admitted feeling just a tad of terror while she'd dragged him down the tunnel.

When she finished, he stood as still as the stone around them. Rachel couldn't see the expression in his eyes. She didn't need to.

"When we get out of here, Russ Taggart isn't going to be able to run far enough or fast enough."

His flat implacability sent shivers skittering along her spine. Folding her arms across her chest, Rachel rubbed her hands up and down her jacket sleeve.

Jake crouched down on his heels and curled a knuckle under her chin. Wincing, she jerked her head back. With a smothered oath, he dropped his hand. The dim light deepened the planes and hollows of his face.

"I owe you, Rachel."

"No, you don't."

"You saved my life. Both our lives."

"Only because I came to first."

"I knew Taggart was following us," he said on a note of scathing self-disgust. "I shouldn't have let the bastard get close to us like that."

"We've already discussed the fact that you didn't see fit to clue me in on your suspicions," Rachel reminded him astringently. "Next time, remember that this is a team effort."

The grim lines in his face eased. "Next time we

go prospecting for forty million dollars and get trapped in an abandoned mine, I will.''

"Speaking of getting trapped..."

Rachel gave the rock wall beside them a quick glance. It was still there, solid, impregnable. Swallowing, she turned back to Jake.

"What do you suggest we do now?"

"Marsh and Shad know where we were headed. We can sit tight and wait for them to come looking for us.''

He swiveled on his heels and aimed the flashlight down the passageway. Darkness swallowed the light whole.

"Or we can see where this leads."

Rachel voted for Plan B. "Sitting around and waiting has never been one of my favorite occupations. Just keep your rifle handy in case we meet up with whatever deposited the pile I stepped in a while ago.''

They didn't meet up with any depositors. Nor did they find a way out. Faced with another solid wall, Rachel wrapped her arms around her waist and shivered in the dank, swirling air.

"We must be close to an air shaft," Jake murmured, playing the flashlight over the walls and ceiling.

One glistening surface in particular caught his

attention. He ran his hand down the slick patch and gave a grunt of satisfaction.

"At least we've got a source for water. We can hold out indefinitely."

Rachel eyed the dark patch dubiously. "What do we do, lick it off the wall?"

"That's easier than spreading a shirt against the rock to collect the moisture, then wringing it out."

"Done that before, have you?"

"Something similar. You learn a lot of ways to soak up spills when you grow up with four brothers."

Judging by his quick grin, Jake was a lot less concerned about their predicament than Rachel. She could only be grateful for the rough and ready survival skills he and his brothers had picked up over the years.

He threw the dark patch another look. "A wet handkerchief has its uses, though. Hold this, will you?"

Handing her the flashlight, he fished a white square out of his back pocket, unfolded it and plastered the cloth against the wall. Refolding the damp fabric, he laid it against her chin.

"Ouch!"

"You've got a helluva bruise there, kid."

"Obviously, you haven't seen what the side of

your face looks like. Here, take the flashlight back and let me clean those cuts.''

To Rachel's relief, his lacerations weren't as deep as she feared. Although the flesh on his temple was purple and puffy, blood had already started to congeal in the cuts. Carefully, she daubed at the red streaks on his face and neck.

''We'd better save the flashlight batteries for emergencies,'' he said when she finished.

Rachel appreciated the need to conserve their light source, but the idea of sitting in the dark for hours, if not days, raised a rash of goose bumps on her arms. Jake, as it turned out, had other plans.

''I'll get a fire going.''

She cast a quick look at the wooden beams supporting the tunnel roof. ''You're not thinking of burning those, are you? One cave-in a day is my limit.''

''No, we've got plenty of fuel on hand.''

''Like what?'' she asked warily, although she had a good idea what that fuel was.

They'd passed a few more piles in their exploration, which had destroyed Rachel's misplaced belief in the theory that animals never soiled their dens. Dried waste would burn, she knew. Man had long gathered dung for fuel. The Plains Indians, in particular, had survived on the vast, treeless stretches by collecting buffalo patties.

That was on the Plains, of course. In the open. With plenty of fresh air to dilute the smoke and the stink. Still, if the choice was between total darkness and a smoky dung fire, Rachel knew which she'd vote for.

Jake, however, reminded her they had ready access to another source of fuel. "I suggest we lug some of those bricks back here. The air shaft will suck up the smoke."

"Good grief! Are you suggesting we burn the money?"

"Why not? Forty million ought to fuel a small fire for a week."

"But…"

"The government can always print more," he pointed out with inescapable logic.

Rachel opened her mouth, then snapped it shut again. The missing millions had cost four men their lives. The damned bills had almost killed her and Jake, as well. She couldn't think of a more fitting use for them.

"You're right. The government can always print more."

By the time they'd transferred the bricks and got the fire going, the pain in Rachel's chin had subsided to a dull ache. Another check of Jake's cuts showed they had crusted over nicely, although he'd

probably need stitches to close them completely
when they got out of the mine...which Jake calmly
insisted they would.

He had no doubt that Marsh would show up before Taggart returned or their situation became extreme. How it could become much more extreme
escaped Rachel, but she was more than willing to
siphon off some of his unshakable confidence
whenever the tunnel walls closed in on her and
claustrophobia threatened.

Somehow, he managed to make the terrifying experience not only endurable, but almost—*almost*—
enjoyable. The terror and tension of the past hour
had eased considerably when they broke open the
paper bricks to build a nest. It almost disappeared
when they snuggled inside. Paper, she had to
agreed, was a great insulator.

So was Jake. Wrapped in his arms, her back to
his chest, her tush nestled on his thighs, Rachel laid
her head against his shoulder. Shadows danced on
the rock walls. The inky scent of newly printed bills
rose around them, obscuring the less pleasant odors
that lingered in the tunnel.

"I never realized our currency had so many prac-
tical purposes besides buying power," she murmured, sniffing appreciatively. "Fuel. Comfy mattress. Room deodorizer. Too bad we can't eat it."

"The ink probably has some nutritional value."

"Ugh! I don't think so! Better be careful, though. New ink like this comes off on your clothes."

The absurdity of her warning hit Rachel a moment later. If she rank ordered everything they had to worry about from one to ten, getting ink smudges on their clothing fell somewhere around minus twenty-two.

The laughter rumbling in Jake's chest told her he'd assigned the matter the same level of concern. For that reason, she considered his suggestion that they remove their clothing with mock deliberation.

"I suppose that's one way to protect them," she agreed solemnly. "You go first."

"Okay."

Their paper nest rustled as he lifted her off his lap and redeposited her atop the crumpled bills.

"You'd better watch it," she warned, grinning. "I might just let you play this game through."

"It isn't a game." Calmly, Jake peeled off his jacket. "It's a matter of survival."

"Survival of the fittest?"

"I was thinking more along the lines of survival of the species."

Good Lord! He was serious! Rachel was still trying to absorb the idea of stripping down and propagating the species when he reached for the zipper on her jeans.

"Jake, this is crazy!"

Dragging down the waistband of her panties, he dropped a kiss on her stomach. "I know."

"We're buried under a mountain, for Pete's sake!"

"I know."

His tongue found her belly button. Rachel's breath hissed out. Tangling her fingers in his hair, she tugged his head up.

"We could be here for days, Henderson."

His eyes gleamed. "If we're lucky."

She couldn't help herself. Dissolving into helpless laughter, she wiggled down until his mouth was within reach of hers.

"This is definitely a first for me," she got out between giggles. "I've never made love on a bed of fifty-dollar bills before."

"We seem to be racking up a string of firsts," he agreed, dropping a gentle kiss on her sore jaw. "One of these days, we've got to go for sheets, blankets and innersprings."

"Do you hear me complaining?"

"No." Less gently, he nipped her throat. "That's one of the things I like best about you, Quinn. I've never heard you complain about anything."

Rachel considered inquiring what he liked least, but decided this wasn't the time to ask. His hands and tongue were too busy and the output from their little fire was too warm. The air in their private cave had definitely heated up enough for them to shed several nonessential layers of clothing.

"Careful," she warned as he shimmied out of his bloodstained vest. "You don't want to open those cuts."

"The hell with the cuts. Come here."

Tangling and trading kisses with Jake in the noisy, tickly nest provided the most incredible sensations. Straddling his lean, muscular flanks some moments later provided even more.

"I think you've toughened me up," she told him breathlessly. "Ordinarily, all those hours on horseback and the ATV would have left me too sore to walk, much less... Oh!"

Gasping, she wiggled her hips to better accommodate the hand he'd slipped between their bodies.

"Funny," he murmured. "You don't feel so tough to me."

"Not right there, I don't!"

He knew exactly where to touch her, how hard to press, how gently to rub.

"Jake..."

The pleasure started too soon, too fast. Jerking up on her knees, Rachel broke the contact.

"Wait!" she panted. "I can't believe this! One touch, and you've got me on the edge of the volcano."

"Good." A smile started in his eyes. "Because that, sweetheart, is where I plan to keep you."

Rachel knew then that she loved him. Like her near climax of a moment ago, it had come on her without warning. She didn't even know when it had happened. Sometime between sliding down into a rocky gulch on her butt and building a nest of fifty-dollar bills, obviously.

Not that it mattered when. All that mattered was that she couldn't remember a time before Jake, couldn't imagine a life without him. Deciding they'd talk about just who was going to keep whom where later, she bent at the waist and lost herself in his kiss.

Chapter 15

Jake stared up into the darkness. Rachel lay against him, sprawled in her usual boneless abandon, arms and legs and clothes tangled with his.

The fire had died. Not from lack of fuel, but because he hadn't wanted to disturb her by feeding it. As long as she was asleep, there was no need to chase the fear from her eyes with the novelty of toasting her toes at a fire fueled by newly printed Federal Reserve notes.

Or with lighthearted lovemaking.

Teasing her into playfulness had taken just about everything Jake had. With every kiss, every touch, he ached at the knowledge that his carelessness had sealed her in what could be her tomb.

How in hell could he have been so damned stupid as to let Taggart get the drop on them! Jake had known the bastard was behind them, had sensed him the way a wild animal senses the hunter. He should have lagged behind Rachel, mounted a rear guard while they were in the mine. Instead, he'd worried that she'd stumble or plunge into a pit and, like a fool, had taken the point.

His gut twisted every time he thought of those moments when they faced Taggart. Jake hadn't exaggerated when he'd told Rachel that Russ Taggart wouldn't be able to run far enough or fast enough if—*when!*—they got out of here.

Jake would get her out. If he had to move those boulders with his bare hands, he'd...

The faint, distant sound jerked him from his grim thoughts. His head came up. The tendons in his neck corded. Every muscle in his body taut, he strained to hear. His first thought was water dripping onto stone. His second, that someone was tapping at the rocks.

Keeping his voice low and urgent, he whispered in the ear placed conveniently close to his mouth.

"Rachel."

"Unngh."

"Wake up, sweetheart."

When he added an insistent prod, she lifted her head.

"Whatimeiz…"

He clapped a hand over her mouth. "Listen."

Eyes wide and frightened, she listened. Her quick little pants dampened his palm. A moment later, he felt her nod. Slowly, he removed his hand.

"Someone or something is out there. I'd better go find out who. Stay here and I'll…"

She gave a soft growl. Jake got the message.

"Right. We're a team. Can you find your clothes in the dark?"

She not only found them, she scrambled into them with a quiet efficiency that won his instant approval. Jake dragged her over for a swift kiss.

"That's another thing I like about you, Quinn," he murmured against her lips. "You don't take a lot of time to get dressed."

"Ha! One of the things I like best about you, Henderson, is that you don't take a lot of time to get me *un*dressed."

He couldn't believe he was grinning when he started down the tunnel.

The tapping grew more distinct with each step they took, but Rachel's pulse was hammering so hard and fast she could barely tell whether the sounds she was hearing came from inside or outside of her head.

Her heart in her throat, she followed the dim path

Jake painted on the floor of the tunnel with the flashlight. He was keeping the beam down and well shielded on the off-chance a thread of light might penetrate the debris blocking the entrance.

He was right to take the precautions, she saw with a leap of excitement that got all mixed up with dread and hope. There, high up in the pile, was a weak glimmer!

"Jake!" she whispered. "Look!"

"I see it."

She forced out her worst fear. "Do you think Taggart might have come back?"

His soft reply didn't reassure her. "If he found his damned container, I figure that's a safe bet."

Rachel figured it was, too. If Russ had found the pod, he would have destroyed whatever evidence could have led back to him. Now, his only worry would be making absolutely sure neither she nor Jake was still alive to counter whatever story he'd concocted to explain his absence and their deaths.

They had their answer several long, agonizing moments later. It came when the sound of a growl snaked through the rock wall to the taut, unmoving listeners. The growl was followed by the scrabble of boots on loose rocks and a startled exclamation.

"What the hell...!"

It was Taggart. Rachel bit back a groan, then jumped at the sound of a pop.

Pistol fire! He was shooting at someone or something! An enraged howl shrieked through the rocks. Stunned, Rachel identified the scream of a wounded animal.

"Sounds like a bear," Jake said in her ear.

"Dear God!"

Two more shots popped off. The howls escalated into roars of rage and pain. Another shriek cut through the tumbled slabs of rock, this one unmistakably human.

She heard a thud, another agonized scream, more shots.

Rachel's skin crawled. From the sound of it, Taggart was engaged in a life-and-death struggle with the animal. Probably the same one that had deposited the mess she'd stepped in earlier.

She'd never felt so helpless, so torn. Taggart had tried to kill her and Jake. Had devised a scheme that led to the death of four aircrew members. Yet Rachel wouldn't wish what was now happening to him on anyone.

The screams on the other side of the rock intensified, so much so she couldn't tell if they were made by man or beast. She stood rooted in place, sickened. Her paralyzed fingers locked on Jake's arm.

"Dear God!"

Jake spun her around, held her face hard against

his chest, as if that would shut out the awful screams. Nothing could shut out the death agony of one of the combatants. Taggart shrieked again, the cry twisting into a final, tortured curse.

Slowly, the howls diminished to savage snarls.

Nausea welled in Rachel's throat. She squeezed her eyes shut, clung to Jake.

Finally, there was only a snuffling, grunting sound. Then that, too, died away.

"What was it?" she whispered, her voice muffled against Jake's chest.

"I don't know. A cougar, maybe. Or a bear."

They didn't find out for sure until several hundred thousand dollars later.

They retreated some distance down the tunnel, rekindled the fire, settled in to wait. Brick after brick went up in flames before a muffled curse had them on their feet and running.

"You think that's Taggart?"

A voice came through the rocks muted and indistinct. "Do you think that's Taggart?"

"What's left of him, looks like," was the laconic reply.

"Shad!"

Jake's bellow bounced off the tunnel walls. Rachel added her shouts to the booming reverberations.

"Shad! We're in here! Can you hear us?"

Boots thudded on rock. Marsh's shout cut through the tumbled slabs.

"Jake! Is that you?"

"Yes! Rachel's here with me."

"Ho-ly Hell, boy!" Shad's voice came through clearer, as if he'd stuck his face right up to a crack. "You two okay in there?"

"Aside from a few cuts and bruises, we're fine."

And the fact that they were trapped on the other side of several tons of rock. Rachel had to bite her lip from shouting out the obvious.

"Who's with you?" Jake yelled.

"It's just me and Marsh. Reece and Evan and Sam are up at the line shack with the team. When Buck Silverthorne told us Taggart had gone off on his own, we figured we'd better come up and warn you."

They'd figured right.

"Guess we should have warned Taggart."

Rachel could almost see Shad pushing his hat forward to scratch the back of his head.

"Poor bastard. Grizzly's pet near about gutted him before the thing died."

She couldn't summon much sympathy for the "poor bastard" at this point. It would come when she and Jake got out.

Maybe.

Marsh pushed all thoughts of Taggart from her head.

"We'll have to get help," he called through the rocks. "All we've got with us is a rusty crowbar we found out in one of the mine sheds."

Rachel sucked in a ragged breath. It would take them five or six hours to reach either the cabin or the lowlands. She could sit in the dark for another five or six hours. She wouldn't like it, but she could do it as long as Jake was beside her.

"Let's try something before you go," Jake yelled to the others. "We can see your light at eleven o'clock high. We've got at least the beginnings of an opening on this side. What does it look like on your side?"

"Like ten tons of rock ready to roll."

Jake swore low and long. There was a scrabble of boots on rock, then his brother shouted through the crack.

"I think I can climb up and poke around without bringing the whole shebang down on my head."

"Be careful!"

The next half hour was the longest of Rachel's life. She could hear Marsh attacking the boulders and debris, counted every chink of his crowbar. His muffled oaths drifted to her, along with Shad's words of caution and encouragement.

Jake dug at the debris with his bare hands until he managed to extract a splintered piece of wood. That in hand, he climbed the piled boulders and scraped at the tiny opening with the makeshift pickax.

Rachel refused to retreat to a safe distance as ordered. Dodging the rock pieces Jake dislodged, she aimed the flashlight up to illuminate his work area. The beam was noticeably weaker, not even as strong as the glimmer of light from the other side. She was devising ways to construct a torch of fifty-dollar bills when Jake's splinter of wood hit the wrong pressure point.

With an ominous rumble that stopped her heart, the boulders above him began to move.

"Jake!"

"Get back!"

"Oh, dear God!"

The sound was so familiar, so horrible. Like a nightmarish audio replay, the awful shriek of stone scraping against each other assaulted Rachel's eardrums. She stumbled back, but not fast enough. The massive rocks bumped and heaved and started down.

Jake came with them. In a flying leap, he sailed over the tumbling boulders. His shoulder smashed into Rachel's, his arm caught her around the waist. Sheer momentum carried them both backward.

Jake slammed into the tunnel's solid rock floor with a force that must have jarred every bone in his body, but kept rolling. Rachel ended up on her stomach, squashed flat under his weight.

The last rumble died. Dead silence thundered in her ears. She let out a shuddering breath. Her muscles went limp. Her toes touched a perpendicular wall of solid rock.

"Jake."

"I'm okay, sweetheart."

"Thank...God."

"How about you?"

"I...can't...breathe."

With a savage oath, he rolled to his knees and patted down her hips, her legs, her ankles, searching for whatever had her pinned. When she finally dragged in enough air to tell him that it was his dive that had slammed every particle of breath from her body, he hauled her up. His savage kiss drove what little air she'd managed to suck into her lungs right out again.

"Glad to see you haven't let a little thing like a cave-in slow you down, big brother."

Marsh's voice floated down. Whipping her head around, Rachel looked up and caught sight of an eye, a nose, a cheek, and half a grin.

Chapter 16

With a groan of unrestrained pleasure, Rachel slid down the sloping back of the huge, claw-footed bathtub until water lapped at her bruised chin.

Fragrant steam rose in clouds around her. Scented bubbles popped and fizzed just under her nose. Lauren had donated the Chanel No. 5 bath gel. Rachel was almost as grateful for the sinfully rich bubbles as she was for the towelettes Sydney had left in the now-pulverized ATV.

Resting her head against the high porcelain tub, she filled her nostrils with the heavenly scent. This was her second bath since departing the copper mine. She was sure it would take two or three more to totally eradicate the stink of rusted iron, decaying wood and printer's ink that had seeped into her pores, not to mention the ink stains she'd acquired in various, embarrassing locations.

Her first dousing had been a hurried one, a quick dunk to get rid of her top layers of dust and dirt before meeting with the small army of police officers and federal agents who descended on the Bar-H. The meetings had gone on all afternoon and well into the evening.

Aunt Alice had arrived in the middle of the sessions. Delivered by Reece and his wife, Sydney, she'd thumped up the flagstones on her walker and demanded to know what in hell had happened up there on the mountain. Evan Henderson and his wife, Lissa, had arrived not a half hour later.

Slightly overwhelmed by the five Henderson brothers ranged around her, Rachel had retold her story for the fifth or sixth time. Jake had finally spirited Rachel away and insisted she rest. At which point Evan had dragged his older brother off, insisting that a physician take a look at the lacerations on his temple.

They were something, the men of the Bar-H. Every one of them handsome as sin. Each leather tough. All fiercely protective of their own. Sam, the youngest, had first captured Rachel's attention, but it was the oldest who'd captured her heart.

Smiling, she raised a toe to catch a drip from the old-fashioned faucet. She could feel her aches and bruises soaking away. Feel, too, the love she'd first recognized in a dark, dank tunnel now filling her with a soft, glorious glow. Jake didn't know how she felt. Couldn't know. They'd never talked of love. The closest they'd come to it was the list they'd started of things they liked best about each other.

She'd add to that list, Rachel mused. She'd spend the week or so before she had to go back to D.C. with Jake, give him time to grow used to the idea of love, find other things to ''like best'' about her. After she went back to work, she could arrange long weekends here in Flagstaff. Or he could come East to see her while he sorted through his feelings.

Rachel didn't kid herself. That might take a while. As Jake had pointed out, he'd been married to Ellen for ten years, had dated her for six years before that. He was still trying to find the part of himself that could exist without her.

He'd find it with Rachel. She knew it as surely as she knew she'd gone searching for lost millions in the rugged mountains and found a treasure beyond worth.

Closing her eyes, she let her head loll back. She'd soak for another half hour. Spin daydreams of Jake. Bask in the warm, happy glow of knowing that he wanted her.

She woke with a startled splash when two arms plunged into water that had gone tepid. Catching her behind the back and under her knees, they lifted her up, out, and against a hard, broad chest.

"I should have known you'd zonk out on me."

"Huh? Whatimeizit?"

"Time to get you to bed, sweetheart."

She came awake fast. Blinking, she barely had time to note the clean white bandage taped to his temple before he carried her out of the bathroom, dripping and slippery with the last of the bubbles.

"Jake, I'm all wet!"

"I'll dry you off," he assured her, heading for the king-sized bed positioned to catch a spectacular view of mountains.

"Your sheets, the mattress, I'll get them soaked!"

"I've waited too long to make love to you on something other than rock or dirt to worry about a little water."

Well, if he wasn't going to worry, she wouldn't, either. She was laughing when he deposited her on the turned-down covers, smiling when he stripped off his clothes, and on fire with need when his long, hard body covered hers.

The sun had set, plunging the room into night. Rachel hadn't noticed either the absence of light or the onset of darkness. Drowsy once more and limp from pleasure, she curled against Jake's side.

"Marry me."

She lifted her head. "What?"

"Marry me, Rachel."

Her jaw sagged. She stared down at him, speechless.

Rolling over, he pinned her to the mattress with a hip. His fingers slid through her still-wet hair, his thumb traced a slow path along her lower lip.

"I know it's too soon. You haven't had time to get to know me. The real me," he added with a ghost of a grin, "not the possible suspect."

"Jake, I... I..."

"I don't want to let go of what we found up there in the mountains. I don't want to let go of you."

"But... Ellen..." Still stunned, she fumbled for words. "Are...are you sure?"

"I'm sure." His hand cradled her cheek. His eyes smiled down at her. "They say real love only happens once in a lifetime. For me, it's twice."

Rachel swallowed a huge gulp of happiness. "Are you trying to tell me you're in love with me?"

"That's exactly what I'm trying to tell you. Marry me, Rachel."

Her answer came straight from the heart. Or maybe it was her gut. Whatever. All she knew was that every instinct in her body shouted this was right.

"Yes."

"Good." He dropped a hard, fast kiss on her mouth, then surged off the bed. "I'll tell Reece to call the preacher. Evan can take care of the license."

Stepping into his jeans, he yanked on the zipper. "We'll have to get blood tests, but I've known Doc Smith all my life. He won't mind if we get him out of bed."

Rachel blinked in sheer astonishment. "You mean now? Tonight?"

"Now. Tonight."

"Jake, are you serious?"

A fierceness came over his face. Leaning down, he planted a fist on either side of her.

"I know what it's like to lose someone you love, Rachel. I almost lost you up there on the mountain. I'm not going to take that chance again."

She had nothing to say to that. Helplessly, she lifted a hand and curled it against his cheek.

"We'll work out the arrangements," he promised with the same unshakable confidence he'd evidenced in the tunnel. "Your job. My responsibilities here at the Bar-H. Who you want to fly in for the ceremony. Where we'll go on our honeymoon. It's all doable, as long as we do it together.''

"You're right," she whispered. "We'll do it together.''

Her wedding day dawned crystal clear. A dusting of snow had been deposited during the night and now sparkled like tears of joy on tree limbs and rooftops. Rachel stretched lazily. Flinging out an arm, she traced the indentations in the pillow next to hers.

Despite the fact she and Jake had made love for most of their prenuptial night, he was already showered and shaved and downstairs making coffee. She'd snatched a few extra minutes to recoup her strength and think through the last minute details.

She'd had all of two days to get ready for the ceremony this morning. With the help of her four soon-to-be sisters-in-law, she'd phoned, shopped, cut and combed. Rachel's family and friends had assembled from all corners of the country.

Jake's extended family had come pouring into Flagstaff, too. His mother, Jess, who'd folded Rachel in her arms and welcomed her into the family with a fierce hug. Lissa's father, Arlen, and old friends of hers from Paradise, Arizona. Lauren's sister, Becky. Various members of Sydney's film crew.

Aunt Alice had arranged for the Downtowner Café to cater the wedding breakfast. Molly and Sam's daughter, Kasey, had spent hours gluing strips of silver and white paper into daisy chains for decorations. Two-year-old Matt and the twins had contributed their frequently vocal input, as well.

Now there was nothing left to do but shower, step into the exquisite creation of creamy lace and white leather she'd found during a frantic sweep through Flagstaff's stores, and join her life to Jake's.

Humming, Rachel had started for the bathroom when a glimmer of metal in a half-open bureau drawer caught her eye. She recognized the corner of a picture frame and slowed her step.

Jake had cleared his belongings off the bureau top and emptied several drawers, stuffing his things into other drawers to make room for hers. They were still working out living arrangements—Rachel had already scoped out a possible job at the government research facility just north of Flagstaff. She didn't care where she lived as long as it was with Jake, and there was no way she was going to take him away from the ranch that was in his blood.

No way, either, she was going to take him away from his memories of Ellen. They were part of him.

Part of what had molded him into the man Rachel loved more with each breath she drew.

Tugging the drawer open a little more, she drew out the framed snapshot. The slight, slender blonde was leaning against a split-rail fence, surrounded by trees that had blossomed with fall gold. She'd tilted her face to the sun. She was young and happy and smiling.

An answering smile softened Rachel's lips. "I'll take care of him, Ellen. I'll take care of the home you guarded for him and his brothers."

Her glance drifted around the room. She'd already left her stamp. Her purse was tossed on the nightstand. Her sweater hung over the foot rail of the massive four-poster. At Rachel's request, Jake had shoved the big, comfy armchair closer to the fireplace so they could snuggle and toast their toes while they watched the late news.

"I might change things around a bit," she told Ellen softly. "I'll probably get into a few arguments. He's pretty hardheaded about some things." Her smile widened. "But you know that, don't you?"

The sound of a door slamming warned her the rest of the house was coming alive. Easing the framed snapshot back into the drawer where Jake had placed it, Rachel went to get ready for her wedding.

She came down the stairs an hour later. Winter-white roses wreathed her upswept hair. A pearl-seeded weskit with long lace sleeves, a scooped neckline, and a fitted bodice hugged her curves before flaring at her hips over an ankle-length, buttery soft leather skirt gored with the same shimmering lace. The scent of Chanel clung to her skin.

The men of the Bar-H were lined up at the bottom of the stairs, ranked in order of seniority. Rachel returned Sam's wide grin, shared smiles with Reece and Marsh, felt a rush of delight at Evan's warm, approving look.

Then her gaze went to Jake, standing tall and tanned and incredibly handsome in a dark blue suit and his best Stetson. The love Rachel first acknowledged in a dark, dank tunnel filled her soul with bright, shining light.

* * * * *

Meet 50 loving dads in

SILHOUETTE® MAKES YOU A STAR!

Look in the back pages of
all June Silhouette series books to find an
exciting new contest with fabulous prizes!
Available exclusively through Silhouette.

Don't miss it!

Silhouette®
Where love comes alive™

P.S. Watch for details on how you can meet
your favorite Silhouette author.

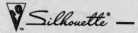

Silhouette®

INTIMATE MOMENTS™
and
BEVERLY BARTON
present:

THE PROTECTORS

Ready to lay their lives on the line, but unprepared for the power of love

Available in March 2001:
NAVAJO'S WOMAN
(Intimate Moments #1063)
Heroic Joe Ornelas will do anything to shelter the woman he has always loved.

Available in May 2001:
WHITELAW'S WEDDING
(Intimate Moments #1075)
Handsome Hunter Whitelaw is about to fall in love with the pretend wife he only "wed" to protect!

And coming in June 2001, a brand-new, longer-length single title:
THE PROTECTORS: SWEET CAROLINE'S KEEPER

Sexy David Wolfe longs to claim the woman he has guarded all his life—despite the possible consequences....

Available at your favorite retail outlet.

Silhouette®
Where love comes alive™